CW00819372

THE DEVIL'S MOUTH

By Nigel Robinson

Based on an original *Baywatch* script, *River of No Return*

BOXTREE

First published in the UK 1993
by BOXTREE LIMITED, Broadwall House,
21 Broadwall, London SE1 9PL

10 9 8 7 6 5 4 3 2 1

Cover and insert photographs: Kim Carlsberg

Cover design by Nigel Davies at Titan Studio

1–85283–847–7

Typeset by DP Photosetting, Aylesbury, Bucks
Printed and bound in Great Britain by
Cox and Wyman Ltd.,
Reading, Berkshire

A catalogue record for this book is available from the British Library.

BAYWATCH™

Life's a beach, and in Southern California the beach is everyone's life.

On the sun-drenched shores of the West Coast of the USA, all of life is dominated by the ocean: at every time of the day or the night the beaches from Ventura in the North all the way down to Tijuana on the American–Mexican border teem with the young (and not-so-young), all of whom have come here to California in search of the good life, or just the best tan ever. After all, when you've got the largest ocean in the world practically on your backdoorstep you might as well put it to some good use.

On weekdays, office workers from town drive down to the beach for a lunchtime swim, and in the evenings young lovers use the ocean as a romantic backdrop to their assignations. Every day surfers ride the foam-topped waves on their customised surfboards looking for the 'big one', the wave that will take them further, higher or faster than the one before; on the ocean itself, away from the beach umbrellas and water-skiers, the rich relax on their luxury yachts, or join the scuba-divers and swimmers exploring the many coves and secluded bays along the coast.

On the golden beaches thousands of people – native Californians or out-of-Staters on vacation – lie in the blistering sun, working on their tans, or simply gazing enviously and longingly at the bronzed and beautiful bodies who have come to Southern California from every corner of the world.

As evening draws on, the beaches become quieter, but you can still hear the delighted cries of midnight surfers, or the crackling of fresh fish being roasted over an open spit at an impromptu beach party.

In fact, to almost everyone who comes to California it seems that the Good Life has packed up, taken all its bags, and moved into permanent residence by the Pacific Ocean.

But, despite its name, the Pacific is one of the most dangerous oceans in the world.

Its deceptively placid waters hide dangerous currents, riptides and undertows which can trap and drown the unwary swimmer; unexpected waves can easily drag a swimmer off-course, or smash him against one of the many broken-down and dangerous jetties along the coast; sharks, too, have been known to intrude into these supposedly peaceful waters, hunting for new meat.

The Pacific Ocean might be the most beautiful ocean in the world: it can also kill you.

If you can turn your eyes away from the ocean for a second, you'll see, dotted along the beach at regular intervals, a series of tall wooden lookout towers. Manning each of these towers, and keeping a constant surveillance on the ocean, are employees of the LA County Department of Beaches.

Dressed in their distinctive red tops and swim gear they keep themselves in peak physical condition and are responsible for saving thousands of lives a year. Hard-working, conscientious and with access to all the most up-to-date and sophisticated life-saving equipment, they are admired throughout the state.

They are the LA County Lifeguards – the men and women of Baywatch.

Prologue

The weather-beaten old man with the grizzled white beard shot a worried look behind him as he navigated the treacherous waters of the river. Shooting down these rapids was a fool's game even at the best of times: one misjudged move, one unexpected current, and a man could be sliced to pieces on the razor-sharp rocks. When you had enemies on your tail it was even more dangerous.

The old man had known these waters, had lived alongside them, for most of his long life, but even he wondered whether he and his kayak – the tiny canoe-like boat he was steering – or the wooden box he was carrying would survive this journey unscathed.

Above the roar of the rapids, and the frantic pounding of his own heart, he could hear the two men yelling at each other.

'Where did he go?' asked a gruff voice.

The old man's heart skipped a beat. He'd done it! He knew this part of the country like the back of his hand: he was sure he'd given those two city hoodlums the slip! *He was a Buchannon after all!*

'There he is!'

Damn it! They've spotted me!

He glanced behind him again to see the two crooks clamber down into their own motor-powered kayak which was moored on the rocky shore.

'C'mon, Lonny! Roll!' the meaner-looking of the two snapped as he and his bearded companion hurriedly prepared to cast off. 'We've got to get him before he reaches Placerville!'

Not if I can help it, you two-bit Al Capones! thought the old man, beginning almost to enjoy the thrill of the chase. With aching muscles, but a stony determination which could have belonged to a much younger man, he sliced his paddle through the rushing waters. First right, then left, then right again. The noise of the turbulent water was now thundering in his ears: he was reaching the most dangerous part of the rapids now: one wrong move and he'd be dead for sure.

'He's heading for the Devil's Mouth!' Lonny cried, as his kayak sped off down the river in pursuit of the old man.

'Crazy idiot!' The mean-looking crook turned to Lonny. 'Well, what are we waiting for? Catch up with him!'

Lonny shook his head nervously: the part of the river which rushed into the entrance of the underground stream known locally as the Devil's Mouth was one of the most dangerous in the whole county: people round here said that if you could get through the channel unharmed then you must have struck a bargain with Old Nick himself.

'No way, Drew,' he said. 'That run's a widow-maker.'

'Shut up, and push water!' Drew commanded, with a menacing look of his eye that promised painful consequences if Lonny didn't obey his orders.

Lonny shrugged and, against his better judgement, powered the engine in pursuit of the old man.

As they cut through the raging waters which poured into the Devil's Mouth the kayak tossed and turned, and it became an effort for them to keep the tiny boat steady. Spray from the turbulent waters soaked them to the skin.

'Can't you keep this damn thing steady?'

barked Drew, as the kayak lurched to one side again.

'Hey man, we're on the rapids!' said Lonny. 'What do you expect?'

Lonny squinted through the wall of spray to catch a glimpse of the old man's kayak, speeding away from them. The old man was paddling his kayak like a demon, he thought; it was hardly surprising, too, when you thought what was at stake.

'There he is!' he yelled. 'Get us closer! He's going right into the Devil's Mouth! Hurry!'

The old man looked triumphantly behind him: his pursuers were gaining on him, but there was no way that they were going to make their way safely through the rocks. It looked like he was gonna win after all!

I'll see ya in Hell, boys! he said to himself, when suddenly a brutal and unexpected current crashed against his kayak, and drove him inescapably down into the waiting Devil's Mouth...

Chapter One

The beautiful blonde down on the beach slowly and sensuously smoothed the sunblock lotion onto her long, shapely legs. Sighing with content, she lay back luxuriously on her beachmat, letting the Californian sun's warm rays caress every perfect inch of her movie-star figure. It was going to be a long, indulgent day on the beach.

'It's a tough job, isn't it, big guy?'

Mitch Buchannon put down his binoculars and shot an evil look at his friend, Eddie Kramer, who was climbing up the steps to the lookout tower.

OK, as supervising lieutenant of the Baywatch lifeguards he was supposed to use the binoculars to keep an eye out for trouble in his patch; but, it was still early morning, the beach was almost empty and – well, the blonde sunbather was something else. There were, after all, some things which a red-blooded divorced American male just couldn't ignore.

'Aha! That's why you assigned yourself the tower this morning!' Eddie said knowingly.

Mitch smiled. 'I just thought I'd remind myself of what I might be missing when the onslaught of summer starts,' he explained, rather lamely.

Hey, even Eddie would have to admit that the blonde was a looker: or rather he would if his pretty blonde girlfriend, Shauni, wasn't following him up to the wooden lookout platform.

Eddie wasn't convinced. 'Wait a minute,' he said. 'How come you're still up here? I thought we were getting a new Supervising Lieutenant to run the headquarters, so that you can go back down to working on the beach?'

'Not yet, at least not until the budget's approved,' replied Mitch.

And, oh boy, it can't come soon enough for me, he thought.

Mitch loved all aspects of his job, but his place was down there on the beach, saving lives, keeping an eye on things and – OK, he had to admit it – occasionally chatting to the beautiful Californian girls working on their tans.

He didn't belong stuck up in a lifeguard

tower, watching out for trouble, and co-ordinating the rescue work like some blasted city hall official. The sooner the new Supervising Lieutenant came, the better!

Mitch looked over to Shauni who was sitting listlessly next to Eddie; she looked pale, and her normally bright sparkling eyes looked red and tired.

'You still feeling sick?' he asked with concern.

Shauni shrugged, and lowered her baby-blue eyes, as though she was trying to hide something. Whatever it was, she wasn't prepared to discuss it with either Mitch or Eddie.

'Why don't you take the afternoon off?' he suggested.

'I'm feeling much better now,' she lied, and added offhandedly: 'It's probably just the shrimp I ate last night.'

'She's been feeling sick ever since Chief Thorpe picked me to go to Australia for a year on the lifeguard programme,' Eddie explained brightly, and gave his girlfriend an appreciative peck on the cheek.

'Go,' she said nonchalantly. 'See if I care!'

Eddie was a great lifeguard, one of the best, and she knew that a place on the elite Australian programme was no more than what he deserved; but it also meant that the two of them would be apart for a whole year.

'I'm sure a very cute Australian lifeguard can take your place here just fine!' she continued. *God, am I ever gonna miss you!* is what she thought.

Shauni's couldn't-care-less attitude didn't fool Eddie for a second. 'Oh, yeah?' he crowed. 'You'd go crazy without me!' He embraced her and nuzzled her ear.

Shauni shot him a look which was meant to say: *If you think I'm gonna miss your blue eyes, that thick dark hair I love to run my fingers through, your 40-inch chest, and the way you always forget to put the cap on the toothpaste tube, then you are really mistaken, buster!* What it actually said was: *God, Eddie, I love you so!*

Eddie leapt to his feet and pointed at his watch. 'Listen, we gotta get outta here,' he told Mitch. 'I'm right next door at Tower Fourteen. If you need any help "watching the water" –' he gave Mitch a knowing all-boys-together wink – 'you let me know and I'll be right here!'

*

'OK, swimmers!' boomed the voice of the swimming coach at Malibu High School. 'On the blocks, please.'

Six well-oiled, muscled students climbed nervously onto the starting podiums at the edge of the school's open-air pool. Ahead, the blue water of the pool, divided into six lanes, shimmered in the sun.

'Get ready!'

Each swimmer leaned forward, arms outstretched, head tucked down. They cast nervous but defiant looks at each other. These swim tests were too important for any of them to screw up; each was determined to be the first to reach the other end of the pool in record time.

'Go!'

The coach fired his starting pistol and the air exploded with cheers and the sound of splashing as six swimmers all hit the water at precisely the same second. Oblivious to everything apart from the swell of the chlorinated water which stung their eyes and the cries from the spectators, the six sliced their path through the water like speeding bullets.

Less than a minute later the winner reached the finish and, with aching muscles, pulled himself out of the water, to a round of deafening applause.

He raised his hand in a triumphal gesture to the crowd, and glanced at the digital clock on the far wall of the swimming arena: 57.21 seconds. Not bad, he told himself: the world record for the 100 metres freestyle was only 10 seconds or so better than that!

'Allll-right!' came the cries from the spectators. 'Brody did it again!'

Matt Brody pulled his wet black hair from out of his eyes and casually acknowledged the cheers. *Hey, maybe all those years of training weren't in vain after all*, the cute-faced seventeen-year-old thought, as he noticed that most of those cheering him on were female.

One of his fellow competitors walked up to him. Clint Chandler had come in second in the race but the two of them were sort of good friends and a friendly rivalry had developed between them.

'Double or nothing?' Clint suggested.

Matt shrugged as if to say, *What the hell?*

Matt wasn't normally a gambling person – after all, his folks were rich and gave him enough money already – but if Clint wanted to go and waste his cash betting on the result of the next race, that was fine by him. Matt had already won quite a tidy sum this morning on their earlier bets.

He nodded and the pair shook hands on the deal.

'OK, breast stroke,' announced the coach. 'On your blocks, everyone – except, that is, Brody and Chandler!'

Matt and Clint exchanged puzzled glances and walked over to the coach who was glaring angrily at them.

'Hey, what's up, Coach?' asked Clint. 'Why can't we join in the next race?'

'If you two "champs" need additional motivation to improve your times,' he said steelily, 'you'd better start thinking about losing races – instead of making bets!'

Betting against the results of sports tests was officially frowned upon at Malibu High: it was the taking part that was important, the teachers insisted rather weakly, not the winning.

Try telling that to the guy who comes in second! thought Clint.

Matt grinned smugly at his friend's downcast expression: 'You listening, Chandler?'

'And that goes for you too, Brody!' the coach reminded him sharply, and Matt's face fell. 'We've got a new swimmer transferring to Malibu High who's won every major meet on the East Coast.'

Matt and Clint listened with interest: if there was going to be more competition on the scene then they wanted to know everything about him.

Coach continued: 'Now, my money says that this' – he looked at his clipboard to check the name – 'this Bobby Quinn is gonna blow both of you guys right outta the water.'

He blew his whistle to signal the start of the next race, and then turned back to the two disgraced swimmers. 'Now, hit the showers!'

'Ever hear of this guy Quinn?' asked Clint, as he and Matt stood under the locker-room showers.

Matt shrugged and applied another squirt of shampoo-conditioner to his collar-length hair.

'He's won all the East Coast meets – big deal,' he said, singularly unimpressed by the new guy's achievement. After all, in Matt's book, if this new guy hadn't swum in the Pacific Ocean, he hadn't really swum at all. Compared to the Pacific the Atlantic Ocean was like a kid's paddling pool!

'Heck, even you could win those, Chandler!' he added dismissively.

Clint ignored the criticism, and returned to his second-favourite subject.

'So put your money where your mouth is, Brody,' he challenged, already having forgotten Coach's earlier reprimand. 'Two hundred bucks says that my time's faster in the lifeguard rookie test.'

'I'm not going out for it,' Matt said, faking disinterest, and started to towel himself dry.

Clint wasn't fooled: he knew that recently the lifeguard rookie tests had been the only thing on Matt's mind. Every year, before the tourists invaded Malibu for the summer, the LA County Beaches and Harbours Authority organised a contest to select young new lifeguards from hundreds of would-be hopefuls. The lifeguard rookie tests were one of the most important events in the beach calendar.

'I thought your old man told you to get a job this summer?' Clint reminded Matt. 'What the hell's better than lifeguarding, huh? You can hang out on the beach all day, you can hustle the babes. You can work on your tan – and get paid for it!'

As far as Clint was concerned, next to becoming the next Kiefer Sutherland or Keanu Reeves, working as a lifeguard on Malibu was probably the most glamorous job in California. The pay might not be as good, but the hours were better, and the perks even greater.

'My old man won't notice *what* I do,' Matt said bitterly, as he tugged on his white Calvin Kleins. 'Besides I don't need the money. I live at the beach. *And* I already got a girl, who's working on *her* tan, hustling *me*!'

Clint sighed, and looked enviously at his friend: a champion swimmer, moody Latin good looks which could knock dead in their tracks half the female population of Los Angeles County, a cute smile, and a father who made thousands every day churning out scripts for the Hollywood film studios – Matt had it all, and he didn't even know it!

Sheesh, Clint thought begrudgingly. *Wouldn't you just know it? Some guys have all the luck ...*

*

Driving west along Santa Monica Boulevard, one of the main highways which cut through Los Angeles, you might be forgiven for thinking that you were in any one of a number of modern-day cities to be found anywhere across the length and breadth of North America.

On either side of you rise tall office blocks, just like the ones you might see anywhere from Dallas to Washington DC, even though the glass fronts of these buildings are glinting dazzlingly in the Californian sunshine. On the sidewalks, street vendors try to impress you with their latest shabby wares, just as they would in New York or Chicago, the only differences here being that these hustlers are making their pitches underneath towering palm trees.

But if you can ignore the smell of hot-dogs and car exhaust fumes, and the sound of angry motorists impatiently honking their horns, you might just catch the distant sound of waves crashing against the shore and the squawking of sea birds wheeling in the cool breeze; or, if you're especially lucky, you might even taste the salt tang of the ocean on the smoggy Los Angeles air.

And then you turn a corner and there it is: the Pacific Ocean, magnificent in its size and *blueness*, and easily the best reason for coming to California.

At least Summer Quinn thought it was.

'Wow,' she gasped, and stood up in the passenger seat to get a better view of the Pacific as her pony-tailed mother steered their blue open-topped convertible off the tree-lined boulevard and onto the boardwalk.

The ocean was even bigger, even *bluer*, than she'd imagined it, and easily ten times more impressive than it had been in any of the beach movies she'd seen as a young kid.

'There it is, Mom, we're finally here!'

Jackie Quinn smiled indulgently at her pretty blonde-haired daughter and drove carefully along the boardwalk. Jackie was a good driver, but the Oldsmobile trailer which they were pulling behind them made driving that little bit more difficult.

'Summer, will you sit down and put your seat belt on!' she scolded, even though she was just as excited as her daughter.

Summer ignored her, and leaned further out of the car. Jackie couldn't say she blamed her: their first sight of the Pacific sure was beautiful.

'Mom, will you just look at the ocean!'

'Summer!'

'C'mon, Mom, let's swim in it!'

Jackie shook her head, even though she was sorely tempted herself by the ocean's blueness. Well, maybe ... No, she told herself, she had to be adult and sensible!

'No, honey,' she said adamantly, 'I want to get to the trailer park and get everything settled before we do anything ...'

'Mom, we've been driving for five days now,' Summer reminded her. 'A couple more hours won't make a difference.' She indicated a large parking lot just off the boardwalk. 'C'mon, Mom, pull in there!'

'Summer, sit down before you fall out!' her mother insisted, as they cruised by a group of surf jocks and their girlfriends who were all heading with their customised surfboards down to the beach.

'Oh God, I have just got to learn to surf!' Summer gushed as she admired the boys' tautly muscled and tanned bodies.

'Summer!' her mother reproved, and then shook her head in good-natured defeat. When her teenage daughter had decided she wanted something, there was nothing in the world which would stop her. And besides, it might be fun!

'OK,' she conceded, 'I'll pull into the parking lot if you sit down – and if you promise to remain seated!'

Summer immediately plonked herself back down in the passenger seat, suddenly the most obedient daughter in the world. She grinned at her mother and planted a grateful kiss on her cheek.

'Mom, you are the best!' she said. 'You are going to be the best thing in Southern California!'

As soon as they had pulled into the parking lot, mother and daughter rushed into their trailer and changed into their swimming costumes. As they changed, Summer looked approvingly at her mom. Jackie was only sixteen or seventeen years older than her daughter, and, unlike the mothers of some of Summer's friends back home, she hadn't let her looks fade away with motherhood. With her long sandy-coloured hair, and almost perfect figure – well, not that perfect: Summer didn't want too much competition for the boys on the beach – she could easily have passed for Summer's older sister.

Jackie's face lit up as she walked across the carpark, hopping as she felt the heat of the tarmac on her bare feet. She squinted in the early morning sun at the rolling waves of the ocean.

'C'mon, Summer,' she said, 'I'll race you down to the beach!'

Laughing and giggling like twin sisters, rather than mother and daughter, Summer and Jackie ran down to the wide and welcoming Pacific Ocean.

As they felt the warm ocean waves splash against their feet, Jackie hugged her daughter close to her. She smiled down at her, and Summer could see the tears of joy in her mother's blue eyes.

'This is a whole new beginning for us, honey, a brand new life,' Jackie said. '*He* is two thousand miles away from us now, and he can't hurt either of us anymore.'

Summer smiled and held her mother more tightly: she knew how much the move to Southern California meant to Jackie. Her mother wiped the tears away from her eyes, and grinned like a little girl.

'OK, honey, let's go for it!'

With an enormous whoop of joy, and a tremendous feeling of release, mother and daughter dived into the ocean.

Summer and Jackie Quinn had arrived in California. And nothing was ever going to make them leave it.

Chapter Two

It was good spending time at home with his young son, Hobie, Mitch decided as the two of them prepared dinner that night in Mitch's bachelor-sized kitchen. Hobie had reached that age when he had grown out of simply hero-worshipping his dad, and now wanted to be treated as his equal. So they found themselves doing everything together – including the cooking – and Hobie's company made a welcome relief from all the stresses and responsibilities of being in charge at Baywatch. In fact, thought Mitch, since the failure of his marriage to Hobie's mother, Hobie had become his best pal in the whole world.

The phone rang and Hobie grabbed the cordless phone before his father could reach it.

'Hello?' he said, and frowned. He offered the

receiver to his father. 'It's some sheriff from somewhere called Placerville,' he said. 'Says it's about your Uncle Alex . . . Who's he?'

'I've got a crazy old uncle named Alex, who lives up on the American River,' Mitch replied as Hobie handed him the phone.

He smiled fondly at the distant memory of the grumpy but affectionate old man, who was always looking to make his first million prospecting for gold, just like one of the forty-niners who had come to California during the last Gold Rush of 1849. As Mitch put the phone to his ear he wondered, with a resigned sigh, just what sort of trouble his old Uncle Alex had gotten himself into this time.

There was a knock at the door and Hobie raced to open it as Mitch took his call. Eddie and Shauni were at the door, and Eddie slapped Hobie's hand in welcome.

'How you doing?' asked Eddie.

'My dad's on the phone,' said Hobie solemnly, indicating that they should be quiet as he led them into the kitchen. 'He's talking to some real important sheriff . . .'

The person on the other end of the phone line identified himself to Mitch as Mister Chen, the sheriff from Placerville, a small town inland, to the south-east of Los Angeles.

'Mister Buchannon,' the Chinese-American

voice crackled over the phone, 'your name and number on the last will and testament identify you as the sole heir to Alex Buchannon who died in a river accident . . .'

Mitch frowned. He hadn't been particularly close to Uncle Alex and had not seen him for years; the way his uncle lived his life, risking dangers a man a third of his age would have baulked at, it was a wonder he'd made it this long. But drowning? There was something wrong there, Mitch thought. Uncle Alex was a top-class swimmer, and, unlike some of the swimmers down on the beach, he knew better than to venture anywhere near dangerous waters.

'He drowned?' Mitch asked the sheriff in disbelief. 'That's impossible. My uncle knew that river like the back of his hand.'

'Unfortunately, this time he took his kayak over a class-five rapid into an area known as the Devil's Mouth,' explained Chen sympathetically. 'Few people come out of there alive . . .'

'Ah, I see,' said Mitch.

It still didn't make sense, though: what would his uncle be doing in such a hazardous place? He shrugged: there were more important matters to take care of first.

'Well, I'll certainly make whatever funeral arrangements are necessary –'

'The Devil's Mouth connects to an underground river,' Chen interrupted, and paused a second before adding finally: 'I'm afraid that anything trapped in it is seldom – if ever – recovered . . .'

The line went dead.

*

'You should have seen Dad the first night,' said Hobie, who was enjoying himself enormously, grossing Shauni out by telling her the story of how Mitch had been stung by a pair of jellyfish when he'd been out in the ocean.

'His whole arm was covered with red welts. It was disgusting,' he said and licked his lips with relish.

Shauni grimaced, but said: 'Hey, what your dad did today was heroic.' She'd been down at Baywatch that day, and knew that Mitch had been stung while out rescuing a girl swimmer who'd also been attacked by the fish.

Hobie shrugged: when he thought about it he supposed it was. However, no matter how many lives Mitch Buchannon saved down on the beach, Hobie could never really picture him as the great hero; to Hobie he was his dad, pure and simple.

Hobie turned to Eddie and changed the

subject. Eddie had told him about his forthcoming trip and Hobie wanted to know everything about the world's smallest continent – well, the important things anyway. 'I hear the jellyfish in Australia are humungous,' he said.

Eddie laughed, and gave Hobie a friendly punch on the shoulder. 'Guess I'll soon find out, won't I?'

'Man,' Hobie whistled in awe. If it was anything like the *Mad Max* films he'd seen on the TV, Australia must be awesome. 'I wish I could go to Australia with you.'

'Eddie wants to go by himself,' Shauni pointed out bitterly, and added sarcastically: 'He wants to have the adventure of his life.'

Without me, she thought, but kept that remark to herself.

Uh-oh, thought Hobie, *something tells me I've made a bad choice of subject here ...*

He was about to change the topic of conversation when his father walked in through the kitchen door. There was a puzzled expression on his face.

'Mitch, Hobie said that a sheriff was on the phone,' said Eddie anxiously. 'What's going on?'

'An uncle of mine just died ...'

Shauni stood up and immediately laid a sympathetic hand on his arm. 'Mitch, I'm sorry ...'

'It's OK,' he replied. 'I haven't seen him since I was a kid ...'

And that, thought Hobie, *was a long, long time ago*.

'He mentioned me in his will though,' Mitch continued. At the mention of the will Hobie's eyes lit up.

'So what did he leave us?' he asked greedily. Hobie hadn't had much experience of wills, but from what he had seen on the TV they usually meant fortunes and title deeds to large expensive estates, or at the very least a lifelong free entry pass to DisneyWorld.

Mitch laughed and ruffled his son's untidy mop of dark-brown hair.

'Don't get too excited!' he cautioned, and Hobie's face fell. 'Uncle Alex was always in debt: it'll probably end up costing *me* money!'

He turned to Eddie and Shauni. 'I'm going to have to go up there and deal with this for a couple of days. Would you do me a favour and look after Hobie for me?'

Eddie and Shauni nodded; they both enjoyed Hobie's company. Maybe he could even help her take her mind off Eddie's forthcoming trip to Australia, Shauni thought.

'Dad, why can't I go with you?' Hobie pleaded. 'I've never been up to the gold-mining country before. And it'd be really cool to go there with you.'

'You really want to go?'

Hobie nodded enthusiastically.

Mitch considered the matter: he saw too little of his son as it was, and it would be nice to spend a couple of days together with him away from the pressures of Baywatch. He decided that the rookie swim trials could get along very well without him and he was sure he could square it with Hobie's teachers to let him off his Friday afternoon classes too.

'OK,' he decided, 'let's go for it!'

'Allll-right!' cheered Hobie, and gave a victory salute.

'Why don't you two guys come along as well?' Mitch asked Eddie and Shauni. 'We could all make a weekend out of it.'

Eddie didn't need to think twice: he'd loved camping ever since he was a kid. He glanced over at his girlfriend. 'How about you? Do you want to go?'

Shauni stroked her chin thoughtfully, and pretended to give the question some serious consideration.

'I don't know – are you sure you wouldn't rather go without me?' she asked only half-jokingly, even though there was a mischievous twinkle in her eyes.

'Come on,' said Eddie, and reached out to fold

her in his loving arms. 'Of course I wouldn't.'

'Then it's settled,' said Mitch. 'First thing tomorrow we're all off to gold-mining country!'

Chapter Three

Mitch rumbled his open-topped blue jeep to a halt on the rocky and bumpy dirt track which led down to the American River and Uncle Alex's cabin in the surrounding foothills. As soon as he had stopped, Hobie stood up on the passenger seat and pointed down to the river, winding like a silvery snake through the brown craggy hills and the green pine trees of California's gold country.

'A thing of beauty, isn't it?' said Mitch. 'That's where they first discovered gold, way back in 1849.'

Hobie indicated the guide book he had in his hands. 'I can read, Dad,' he said loftily.

Mitch shrugged and drew their attention down to the river. In the distance a tiny figure in a red kayak was riding the rapids. 'Wow!

Check that one out!'

The kayak was twisting expertly in and out of the swells and currents, skipping like a stone over the turbulent waters, as though it was one with the river itself. Whoever the pilot was, Mitch decided, he sure knew his stuff, and the confidence with which he ploughed through the water with his twin-bladed paddle was impressive.

The kayak drew nearer and now he could see the pilot's red helmet and bulky blue lifejacket concealed the figure of a shapely and very attractive young woman. Even though he couldn't see her face, Mitch grew even more interested. The kayak sped past them and headed on down the river.

Suddenly an unexpected cross-current smashed into the tiny craft, and it turned upside down, sending its pilot into the cold icy water.

Hobie gasped and grabbed his father's hand urgently, but Mitch assured him that there was nothing to worry about: this pilot was obviously an expert and she'd get out of trouble in seconds.

'Watch how she recovers,' he said, and within seconds the kayak rolled over and righted itself, with the woman still firmly seated in the cockpit. It was a perfect Eskimo roll, he reflected admiringly. With a mighty sweep of her paddle she resumed, heading off at full-speed down the river.

'Oh, beautiful, that was just beautiful,' enthused Mitch, and was suddenly aware of the eyes of Hobie, Eddie and Shauni all looking accusingly at him.

'Er, I'm talking about the river...' he said unconvincingly, and flushed red with embarrassment.

Eddie grinned. 'Yeah, right...'

'Sure, Dad,' the worldly-wise Hobie tut-tutted, and shook his head. Really! For someone who was nearly forty his dad was letting his hormones get way out of control: if he didn't get his act together soon Hobie was going to have to go out and find him a girlfriend to keep him in line!

Mitch looked to Shauni for support, but she just smiled: really at times men were just so pathetic – she didn't know why she loved them so much!

*

When they finally reached Uncle Alex's cabin, Chen, the grey-haired sheriff from Placerville, was waiting for them. After introducing himself to Mitch's party the innocuous-looking little man warned them to be prepared for an unpleasant surprise. When the sheriff creaked open the old wooden door to the cabin Mitch whistled with amazement.

Burglars had broken into the cabin and had turned it inside out, wrecking whatever they could find. Drawers had been pulled out of cupboards and sideboards and their contents rifled through before being strewn over the floor; chair cushions had been ripped open, floorboards prised up, and the glass of Uncle Alex's trophy cases smashed; pages had been torn out of notebooks and scrunched up and thrown on the floor.

Mitch noticed the silver cups which Uncle Alex had won as a youngster in the swimming and kayaking championships. They were obviously valuable, but for some reason the burglars hadn't taken them. Following a hunch, he went over to one of the opened drawers: a wallet full of dollar bills had also been left untouched. Mitch wondered if, in fact, the burglars had taken anything at all.

It was obvious to Mitch that this break-in hadn't been the work of an average burglar. Whoever had wrecked the cabin had been looking for something specific. But what could it be? And, more to the point, had they found it?

'Since your uncle's cabin now belongs to you, Mister Buchannon,' Chen continued in his soft

Chinese-American lilt, 'I'm afraid you're responsible for the clean-up ...'

'Any idea who trashed the place?' asked Eddie, as he started to help Shauni tidy up some of the mess.

Chen shook his head sadly. 'I had a forensic team brought down from Sacramento,' he said. 'There are no fingerprints, no hair, no blood, no evidence whatsoever.'

'They must have been professionals then, whoever they were,' figured Shauni.

'Yes,' agreed Chen, 'and, what's more, the cabin was apparently ransacked *after* Alex Buchannon's death.'

Puzzled, Mitch scratched his head. 'None of this makes any sense,' he said. 'Sure, Uncle Alex prospected for gold all his life, but he never found more than two nuggets. And why didn't the burglars take his trophies, or his money?'

'So what do you think they were after?' asked Shauni. Mitch had to admit that he hadn't the slightest idea.

Chen stepped forward. 'A week before he died, Alex was apparently drunk –' Chen began carefully.

'So?' It was no news to Mitch that his uncle occasionally liked a little too much of the local hooch.

'Well, he started bragging that he'd found

"The Boot" …'

'The *what*?' asked Eddie, exchanging blank looks with Mitch and Shauni.

Hobie quickly rustled through the pages of his guide book.

'Big Foot, Big Rock … – Here it is – "The Boot"!' he said. 'It's the biggest gold nugget ever discovered during the Gold Rush. Here, see –' He handed Eddie the guide and pointed to the relevant entry. 'It was shaped like a cowboy boot and was just as big. It's worth millions!' He looked at Chen. 'And Uncle Alex found it?' he asked breathlessly.

Mitch urged his son to calm down. 'I wouldn't count on it, Hobie,' he cautioned. 'Uncle Alex used to brag that he'd found everything from the Lost Dutchman Mine to the Treasure of the Sierra Madre.' Mitch laughed, and tapped the side of his head with his index finger. 'He was nuts!'

Eddie continued reading the article on The Boot. 'It says here that the Golden Boot was stolen during the Tong Wars and hasn't been seen since the 1850s.'

'Tong?' asked Hobie. 'What's a Tong?'

'A Chinese secret society,' explained Shauni. 'They came with the other Chinese when they arrived in California, attracted by the rumours of gold, and to work on the trans-continental railroad. Isn't that right, Mister Chen?'

The Chinese-American coloured slightly; most law-abiding members of the Chinese community didn't like being reminded of the criminal activities of the Tongs. They were something of which most Chinese weren't particularly proud.

'That's quite correct, Miss McClain.'

'According to this, the Golden Boot was supposedly buried somewhere along this very river,' Eddie continued reading, and then looked up seriously at Hobie. 'I suppose he *could* have found it ...'

'I'm afraid that that's just a rumour which too many people would like to believe,' said Chen in a superior tone which seemed to suggest that Eddie shouldn't encourage Hobie in his wild speculations. As far as Chen was concerned the story of the Golden Boot lay somewhere in the same category as the reported sightings of the legendary Big Foot, the alleged existence of the Loch Ness Monster, or the integrity of a Hollywood lawyer.

Eddie ignored him. 'Well, maybe it is true,' he suggested. 'Maybe Mitch's uncle really did find something this time.' He indicated the broken furniture: 'I mean, why would someone tear up his cabin like this?'

Chen turned to Mitch. 'I was rather hoping

that you'd be able to answer that question, Mister Buchannon,' he said. 'Your uncle left you something else in his will. It's in my car ...'

Wondering what it might be, the four of them followed the sheriff outside. So interested were they in Uncle Alex's mysterious final gift to his nephew, that they all failed to notice the late-afternoon sunlight which glinted off a pair of binoculars a little way off in the trees.

They didn't know it but they were being watched.

Sheriff Chen reached into the glove compartment of his car and pulled out a dirty envelope which he handed to Mitch. Mitch tore open the envelope and cast his eyes over the official-looking paper inside.

'Come on, Dad,' urged Hobie, caught up in the excitement. 'Tell us what it says!'

'"I also bequeath to my nephew, Mitch, all objects of value concealed in our secret spot which is known only to him ...",' Mitch read out.

Wow! thought Hobie. *This is getting more like an episode of* The Hardy Boys *every minute!*

'What secret spot, Dad?' he asked eagerly. 'Where is it?'

Mitch's brow furrowed and he shook his head. 'Sorry to disappoint you, Hobie,' he said, 'but I have absolutely no idea.'

Chen regarded Mitch through narrow inscrutable eyes.

'Are you sure you're not just trying to keep this "secret spot" known only to yourself, Mister Buchannon?' he asked suspiciously.

There was something mildly disconcerting about the Chinaman's tone: Chen seemed just a little too eager to know the whereabouts of Uncle Alex's secret spot. Mitch couldn't escape the nagging feeling that Chen knew considerably more than he was admitting.

'Sheriff, the last time I saw my Uncle Alex I was Hobie's age,' he replied. 'I haven't got the slightest idea what he's talking about!'

'Well, maybe being back here will trigger off some memories for you,' suggested Chan, suddenly his old amicable self again.

He looked up at the sky. 'It's going to be dark pretty soon: we'd better get back to town.'

Hobie glanced up at his father. 'I'd kind of like to camp out here,' he said. 'Like, I never knew Uncle Alex or anything, but it sure would be cool.'

'Sure, why not?' said Mitch. He looked enquiringly at Chen. 'It's OK to camp out here, isn't it?'

'It's your property now, Mister Buchannon,' the sheriff replied tersely. 'You can do with it what you like.'

Shauni walked over to Eddie and took him

firmly by the arm. 'Well, we are going to stay in that cute little bed-and-breakfast we saw in town,' she announced.

'Wait a minute, it might be fun,' Eddie said. 'It could be romantic, y'know, sleeping out under the stars ... We could zip ourselves up into a bag ...' He winked suggestively at Shauni, who turned away haughtily.

'Zipping myself up in a bag on the ground with insects and spiders creeping and crawling all over me is not my idea of romance, OK?' she said curtly.

Eddie was about to suggest that, if he had his way, it was going to be him doing the creeping and crawling all over her, but Shauni hadn't finished yet.

'I prefer a four-poster bed at the inn we saw on the way here,' she said and gave Eddie a teasing look: 'But *you* can stay wherever you want.' She skipped off towards the jeep. 'See you, guys.'

Eddie looked helplessly at Mitch and Hobie: it would be great fun spending the night out in the wilds with the guys. Then he looked back at Shauni, and sighed. Eddie knew when he was beaten. He held up his hand in a gesture of defeat and followed Shauni to the jeep.

'Hey, what can I say? I'm sorry, Mitch.'

Mitch grinned; Shauni could twist Eddie

around her cute little finger – and how he loved it!

'No contest, Eddie,' he chuckled. 'No contest at all!'

Chapter Four

Eddie felt Shauni's warm firm body pressed tightly against him, her full lips touching his with unchecked desire. He ran his hands down the small of her back and she shivered with delight. Suddenly she broke away from the passionate embrace, and headed for the bathroom door of the hotel room they had booked into.

'What's up?' he asked. Had he gone and done something wrong?

'Nothing,' she replied moodily, and locked the bathroom door behind her. 'I'll be right back,' she called from inside.

Eddie sat down on the bed and shook his head despairingly. These past few days he found he couldn't get through to Shauni at all. It was as though she was hiding something from him.

And her violent changes of mood – up one minute, and down the next like a damn yo-yo – were driving him crazy! What had gotten into her?

Five minutes later Shauni emerged: if Eddie didn't know her better he would have sworn that she had been crying.

'What's wrong?' he demanded.

'Nothing,' she lied, and averted her eyes.

'Oh yeah? You go in there five minutes ago with a negligée, and now you come on out with an attitude,' Eddie pointed out angrily. 'Now what's up?'

'I don't have an attitude, Eddie,' said Shauni, her voice positively oozing with attitude.

'Shauni, a couple of minutes ago you were kissing me like there was no tomorrow ...'

'If you go to Australia then there won't be a tomorrow, will there?'

Aha, so that's it!

'I see ...' said Eddie, and lightened up a little: 'Look, Shauni, if I go to Australia it'll only be for a year, that's all ...'

'Oh, that's all?' was Shauni's indignant response. 'Just a year?'

Hey, chill out, she muttered sarcastically to herself. *That's only three hundred and sixty-five days, or 8,750 hours! I mean if you really want to make yourself miserable, Shauni, try think-*

ing of it as only 525,600 minutes, or just 31,536,000 seconds!

'*Just* a year?' she repeated aloud. 'A lot can happen in less than a year, Eddie . . .'

Eddie stood up from the bed and reached out to embrace her. 'If two people love each other, then they should be able to work something out,' he reasoned.

Shauni shook her head. Eddie was just like all men, she decided: when it came to love he hadn't the faintest idea what he was talking about!

'Be halfway around the world from each other and still remain committed?' she scoffed.

Eddie looked the girl he loved straight in the eyes. 'Yes,' he said with conviction.

Shauni returned his gaze. 'I'm talking *real* commitment here, Eddie . . .'

Eddie frowned. Real commitment? What was she talking about?

*

While Eddie and Shauni wondered about the future of their relationship, Mitch and Hobie were sitting in front of a roaring fire, frying steaks in the open air outside Uncle Alex's hut.

In the sky overhead they could see the Great Bear shining down on them, and the air was filled with the croaking of the frogs down by the river, and the crashing of the water as it rushed its way downriver, through the rapids and into the Devil's Mouth.

In this part of the county the river was like the beach at Baywatch, Mitch decided: it was central to your way of life and wherever you went its sounds formed a constant inescapable counterpoint to your existence.

'C'mon, Dad,' urged Hobie, who was impatiently waiting for his steak. 'You must remember something about Uncle Alex!' *Hey, his dad might be nearly forty now, but he should still have all his brain cells on him!*

'Hobie, I was just a kid,' Mitch said in his defence.

The truth was that Mitch's memories of Alex had become so mixed up with all the wild tales the Buchannons had told about the black sheep of their family that he no longer really knew where the truth ended and the apocryphal stories began.

'There must be something you remember!' Hobie persisted. 'Right – let's start with basics! What did he look like?'

Mitch thought hard, and slowly called to mind the appearance of his old uncle. But it wasn't his grinning white-bearded face that he recalled, but something else. He smiled at the memory.

'The thing I remember most about Uncle Alex were his hands,' he began, and Hobie frowned until his father continued: 'He had these enormous callouses on both of his hands from swinging picks and shovels,' he said. 'He once told me that the best way to get rid of all those callouses was by rubbing gold dust between your hands.'

Now at last this was getting interesting! decided Hobie.

'So, Dad, when you came up to visit him, did he ever find any gold?'

'Once,' Mitch replied and chuckled as Hobie's jaw dropped in amazement. 'One day we went downriver,' he continued, pointing down to the American River which could be clearly seen from Uncle Alex's cabin. 'For hours we panned for gold.' He laughed as the memory came flooding back. 'Of course, all we got was dirt, rocks and sunburn.'

'Of course ...' said Hobie, disappointed.

'So I said: "C'mon, let's get home, I'm tired."'

Hobie looked even more dismayed: what a wimpish thing to say!

'But Uncle Alex, he says: "No, wait, it's the end of the day – you always get lucky at the end of the day. Let's try just one more time ..."'

'So what happened?' asked Hobie enthusiastically. By now he was getting deeply involved in his father's tale.

Mitch raised his hand as if to say that Hobie needn't worry: he was finally coming to the point of his story.

'So I went back down to the river with the pan and put it in the river. I rolled it around and around, and then washed off all of the water and dirt and – what d'you know? – there it was. In the bottom of my pan, a tiny gold nugget!'

'What, you mean like *real* gold?' Hobie gasped.

Mitch nodded. 'That's right, Hobie – real gold.'

Before Hobie could ask why his father wasn't a millionaire by now, and why they weren't living the life they should have been accustomed to, Mitch continued: 'Now I'm sure that Uncle Alex actually put the gold there in my pan – but it was still real gold.'

Hobie was really impressed. He wanted to ask where Uncle Alex had found the gold he'd put into his dad's pan, and where it was now; he wanted to know if there were any more gold nuggets still to be found in the surrounding countryside; he wanted to know the current value of gold against all the world's major currencies.

All he managed to say was: 'Wow!'

Mitch laughed; Hobie was rarely rendered speechless: he could tell he was really impressed.

'Real gold?' Hobie asked again, as if he didn't quite believe what his father was telling him.

'That's right, real gold,' Mitch confirmed, and smiled as he recalled his own similar excitement at finding the minuscule nugget in his pan.

Then he frowned as a long-forgotten memory slowly came to the forefront of his mind. 'Wait a minute . . .' he said.

'What's up, Dad?'

Mitch closed his eyes, casting back in his mind for that long-past day when he and Uncle Alex had gone out gold-prospecting. *Just what was it that the old man had told him that day?*

'Uncle Alex suggested that we take the piece of gold and put it into a pouch – and then hide it in a secret spot so that no one would ever be able to steal it.'

'And did you find a secret spot?' asked Hobie, wide-eyed.

'Yeah, we did,' his father said, and then shook his head in frustration. 'But it was years ago, Hobie, I've no idea where it is now.' He shrugged. 'It must be downriver someplace.'

Hobie jumped to his feet. 'Well, c'mon!' he said determinedly. 'Let's go look for it! Maybe

Uncle Alex hid the Golden Boot there.' He tugged at his father's sleeve. 'Come on, Dad!'

'It's the middle of the night, Hobie,' Mitch pointed out. 'Sit down!'

Hobie pulled a face: didn't his dad have any sense of adventure left? Nevertheless he did as he was told.

'I'll tell you what,' said his father. 'When Eddie and Shauni get here tomorrow morning with the jeep we'll all go downriver and look for that secret spot.'

'All right!'

Mitch removed the frying pan from out of the fire, and slipped it onto a plate, but his mind was elsewhere – somewhere along the river, in Uncle Alex's secret place.

Back at the beach, he thought, they'll be running the first trials for rookie lifeguards tomorrow. But here in gold-mining country, if they found the Golden Boot, by tomorrow he and Mitch could be millionaires!

Chapter Five

The following morning Jackie steered her long blue convertible into the parking lot beside the beach, and gazed out at the sparkling turquoise ocean: somehow she knew that, no matter how long she stayed in California, she'd never lose her appreciation of its beauty.

Even though it was still early, the surfers were already riding the ocean waves, and eager sun-worshippers had staked their claim to their favourite parts of the beach. Down by the sea a group of students from Malibu High were playing a game of basketball. Youth, fun, and excitement, thought Jackie: this was what California was all about.

The main headquarters of the lifeguard department of the LA County Beaches and Harbour Authority was on the beach, and a long queue of teenagers had already formed outside the building even though it wasn't due to be opened for at least another hour. Today was the first day of the official tests to decide which of hundreds of eager young Californian hopefuls would be chosen as trainee lifeguards for the coming summer months.

'I told you we were going to be late, Mom!' complained Summer in the passenger seat, as she counted the scores of people already in the queue, each of them wearing Speedos or one-piece swimming costumes. Everyone was deeply tanned as only native South Californians can be.

'Look how buffed those people are,' she gasped with envy. 'They've probably been swimming in the ocean all their lives! I hadn't even seen it till yesterday!'

She glanced over at her mother who was inspecting herself in the rearview mirror. Summer suspected she hadn't been listening to a word she'd been saying. Jackie adjusted her long ash-blonde hair in the mirror, and took another long critical look at herself.

'Honey, do you think I look all right?' she asked nervously. 'And this dress – you don't think it's too tight?'

She smoothed the creases of the spangly blue dress, and looked doubtfully at it: did it reveal too much? Or did it reveal too little? Back home, Jackie had been a successful lounge singer and today she was going to an audition for a singing job she'd seen advertised in the latest edition of *Variety*. She knew it was essential to make a good initial impression on the judges if she stood any chance at all of getting the job.

'You know, I wore this dress when I was singing over at the City Bowl Lounge, and it went down really well.'

'I might as well not even sign up,' Summer moaned as she studied the people in the queue.

All the boys were strong and muscular, with well-developed biceps and pectoral muscles, and firm tight buns; the girls were as sleek and as glamorous as movie stars, with not a spare ounce of fat between them. Everyone looked as if they had been swimming in the Pacific since the day they were born.

'They're probably gonna hate it,' Jackie decided gloomily, and continued to examine the dress.

Back in Pittsburgh, her blue dress had made quite an impression on the diners in the nightclubs in which she'd sung, but this was California and tastes here were bound to be different. What might have been thought of as racy or sophisticated back home would probably be regarded here as being suitable only for one of the bag ladies down on LaBrea.

Summer turned back to her mother and smiled encouragingly.

'They are going to love it, Mom,' she reassured her, and opened the passenger door of the car. 'You'll knock 'em dead!'

Jackie kissed her daughter's cheek. 'Make new friends, honey,' she said. 'I love you.'

'Love you too, Mom,' said Summer and ran over to join the queue of would-be rookie lifeguards.

Sitting astride his motorbike, Matt Brody cast an admiring glance her way as she passed: in fact, it would have been difficult not to notice Summer, even if she hadn't been as attractive as she was. Her pale Pennsylvanian skin was about as out of place among all the tanned beauties on the beach as a touch of self-effacing modesty would be in Madonna's latest press releases. He took off his Ray-Bans to take a better look and gave an appreciative whistle before turning back to Clint.

'So,' he said, getting back down to business, 'which one of those guys do you think is Bobby Quinn?'

Clint shook his head and gave Matt a 'search-me' expression: not one of the guys in the queue looked as if he could be the champion swimmer from the East Coast.

'Keep checkin' them out,' he said. 'That guy's gotta be here someplace. I want to know what the competition's like!'

Summer joined the end of the queue and brightly introduced herself to a dark-haired girl who was also hoping for a place as a rookie.

'Do you know how many rookies they're gonna take on this year?' she asked.

'Ten – maybe twelve,' the girl, who said her name was Tanya, replied.

'That's it?' gasped Summer, and looked at the long line in front of her. There were going to be a lot of disappointed people by the end of the day, she decided: she just hoped that she wasn't going to be one of them.

'That's right.'

'So how do they decide who's going to make the grade?'

'They have tests and interviews,' Tanya explained. 'But mostly it's the strongest swimmers who make it into rookie school. And even then only half of them are going to make it out.'

Summer was impressed: she hadn't realised just how exacting the standards were to qualify as a lifeguard at Baywatch. At the same time she was determined to give it her best shot: becoming a lifeguard had been one of her dreams ever since she had been a child, fooling around in the local swimming pool back home, and admiring the cool, reassuring presence of the lifeguards there.

A gruff masculine voice behind Summer said: 'Well, I knew it would be either sing or swim . . .'

Summer spun around on her heels to see a tall imposing unshaven man in his mid-forties smiling at her.

'Jed!' she cried, in a voice which suggested to her new friend, Tanya, that the meeting wasn't exactly a welcome one. She led Jed away from Tanya so she wouldn't hear their conversation.

'Suddenly everyone wants to run off chasing their dreams,' Jed drawled, still smiling, even though there was now an angry, dangerous glint in his weaselish eyes.

'Well, I've chased mine clear across the country. And now that I've caught it, I swear I ain't never letting it go, baby!' He reached out and grabbed Sumer's arm, who angrily shook it aside.

'Jed, my mother doesn't want to see you any more,' she said as assertively as she could.

Summer would never admit it but Jed had always scared her, especially when he'd been drinking; even this early in the morning she could smell the tell-tale whiff of cheap gut-rot whisky on his breath.

'Well, then, ain't she gonna be surprised when she sees me?' he said sarcastically, and reached for Summer's arm again. 'Now, where did you park the trailer? I'll drive you there and we can wait until she gets home.'

'*Just leave us alone!*' Summer cried, and was suddenly aware that a small crowd of swimmers had gathered around her and Jed.

'Hey, what's going on?' asked Tanya.

Matt stepped forward, and angrily pushed Jed away from Summer.

Ignoring Jed, he looked enquiringly at the pretty blonde teenager. 'You want me to butt in or out?' he asked.

'In,' replied Summer firmly.

'This hasn't got anything to do with you,' Jed said to Matt.

Matt stepped forward and raised a threatening fist at the older man. 'It does now,' he stated flatly. 'It's got to do with me and all of my buddies here!'

Jed took a wary look at Matt: if Jed had been younger he wouldn't have thought twice about teaching the punk a lesson; as it was he wouldn't last a minute in a fight with the firmly muscled seventeen-year-old.

All right, kid, you might have won the first round but ...

He glowered at Matt and then turned back to Summer.

'OK, I'll go now,' he said, 'but you tell Jackie

I'm here to stay!'

After Jed had stormed off up the beach, Matt introduced himself to Summer.

'Thanks for the help,' she said gratefully. 'That could've turned nasty.'

'Who the hell was the dork?' asked Clint.

'Jed – my mother's ex-boyfriend.'

Damn! thought Summer. *Why did he have to track us down and come and louse up our lives? Just when me and Mom are finally getting our act together without him!*

Chapter Six

Hobie woke up early and was washed, dressed and down in a secluded shallow spot by the river before Mitch had even dragged himself out of his sleeping bag. He had taken a gold prospecting pan from Uncle Alex's cabin and was using it to scoop up water and earth from the riverbed, eagerly looking for any tell-tale flecks of gold dust.

Mitch had spent the rest of the previous night telling Hobie tales of the original 'forty-niners' who had arrived in Southern California during the last century, all in search of the gold that had just been discovered there. All of them had bought small patches of land – often sold to them by sharks and crooks – and, without any geological knowledge, hoped that there would be a lode of gold hidden underneath the surface, just waiting to be unearthed.

Most of these early prospectors went away empty-handed, but for the lucky few the discovery on their land of a lode of gold, no matter how small, meant undreamt-of riches. Hobie had figured that, as Uncle Alex's land now belonged to his father, if there were any undreamt-of riches going here, then he deserved his fair share.

Concentrating hard, Hobie swirled the muddy water around the pan, trying to separate the earth from the gold nuggets he was convinced he would find. He frowned. All he could see was a nasty mess of sludge and slurry – not a nugget of gold to be seen!

Behind him he heard a man chuckle and he quickly turned around. A swarthy, mean-looking man had crept up on him without a sound, like a cat.

'You're swirling it around too fast, son,' he volunteered. 'You gotta scoop up a pan of screen and come straight up with it.'

He took Hobie's pan from him and showed him how to gently tilt it this way and that, slowly sieving off a little bit of earth at a time.

'And then you get it between you and the sun, and swirl the slag off nice and easy like,' he continued, 'until you see the gold kicking up light at you!'

Hobie looked at the emptied pan eagerly, and his face fell: there wasn't even a speck of gold-dust in the pan.

'Well, better luck next time,' the stranger said philosophically.

Nevertheless, Hobie thanked him for his first valuable lesson in gold-prospecting.

'Hey, you're welcome,' grinned the man, revealing his blackened and chipped teeth. 'My name's Drew – what's yours?'

'Hobie Buchannon.'

'Buchannon!' Drew repeated: he obviously recognised Uncle Alex's family name. 'That's a good name in these parts. Are you and your old man planning to go downriver today?'

'I hope so,' he replied, briefly wondering how Drew knew that he was here with his dad. He heard Mitch's voice calling for him.

'I'm over here, Dad,' Hobie shouted, and Mitch came running bare-chested down the river.

'Hey, what's going on?' Mitch asked, as he wiped the last patches of shaving foam off his jaw with a towel.

'This guy's teaching me how to pan for gold,' Hobie explained, and turned around to introduce Drew to his father.

'Huh? What guy?'

At the sight of Mitch, Drew had disappeared,

just as silently as he had arrived.

*

After Eddie and Shauni had arrived from their bed-and-breakfast, Mitch had piled all their gear into the jeep and driven them a few miles downriver to a place where they could hire a raft and sailing equipment. Mitch had phoned ahead and spoken to Jim and Peter, the two men who ran the camp, and they had promised that they would get one of their very best river guides to take them on their trip over the rapids.

As Mitch and Hobie went to organise the equipment, Eddie took Shauni aside.

'Are you sure you want to do this?' he asked her.

'Why?' she teased. 'Would you rather go without me?'

'Would you please stop saying that?' Eddie snapped. Ever since he'd gotten the chance to go to Australia, Shauni had been making these sly little cracks, and they were beginning to annoy him. Eddie knew the separation was going to be hard for her but, hell, it wasn't going to be so easy for him, either.

Shauni apologised, and Eddie continued: 'What if you were to get sick again this morning?'

This morning had been the third in a row, when Shauni had spent a good ten minutes throwing up in the bathroom. This time she had blamed it on the salmon pie they had eaten last night at a restaurant next door to the bed-and-breakfast place.

'Don't worry,' she reassured him, and suggested that they rejoin Mitch and Hobie. 'I'm going to be just fine.' Deep down inside, Shauni hoped that she sounded convincing enough.

'You're all going to have a great time,' Jim was telling Mitch and Hobie. 'The South Fork Rapids are some of the best you'll find. And your guide is one of the best there is around here.'

'Great,' said Mitch, 'because we're not looking for class one or two rapids here.' He winked at his son. 'We want fours and fives, don't we, Hobie?'

'Too right!' he said, and slapped his father's hand.

Just then they heard the mournful wail of a badly played saxophone coming from somewhere down on the riverbank.

'What's that?' Mitch asked, and grimaced: whoever was playing the sax sure wasn't going to give any professional musician any sleepless nights.

Peter laughed: 'Casey Jean's learning how to play the saxophone.'

Casey? Casey Jean? Mitch and Hobie looked at each other with surprise.

'She's gonna be your guide,' Peter explained, not noticing the Buchannons' expressions. 'Maybe you know her? She used to be a beach lifeguard in LA before she came down the river.'

'You say her name's Casey Jean?' asked Mitch. 'CJ?' Peter nodded, and Mitch grinned even wider.

He remembered the long-legged blonde with the baby face from way back, when she worked at Baywatch. He also remembered the devastating effect that CJ had on men. Peter pointed to the solitary figure playing the sax by the river's edge. With a mischievous little-boy grin Mitch indicated that the others should remain silent, and he tiptoed over to where CJ was playing.

So intent was CJ on trying to coax something even vaguely tuneful out of her instrument that she didn't hear Mitch creep up behind her.

'You'd better hope there aren't any love-sick moose around,' he whispered into her ear.

With a shriek of surprise CJ turned around, hitting Mitch full-square in the chest with her saxophone.

'Oh my God!' she cried as, with a yell, Mitch

tumbled head-first into the river.

'Oh, Mitch, I'm so sorry,' she managed to say through howls of laughter, as Mitch flailed about helplessly in the shallow water, gasping for breath in the icy coldness of the river. 'I was just so surprised to see you standing there!'

Mitch gazed up ruefully at CJ's smiling face. 'Not as surprised as I was,' he spluttered.

'Here,' CJ reached out her hand. 'Let me help you out.'

When Mitch had been pulled out of the water, he hugged CJ in welcome. 'It's been a long time,' he said. 'How are you, CJ? How's Larry?'

The temperature dropped rapidly, as CJ stood up and fixed Mitch with a stare so frosty that it could have frozen up the river itself.

Uh-oh, thought Mitch, *I definitely said the wrong thing there...*

'Mitch Buchannon, if you dare to mention that name again you're going right back into that river,' she said – and meant it.

'Not again, huh?' asked Mitch, and tutted sympathetically.

CJ nodded stoically. 'Yes, again.'

CJ was an extremely attractive woman and she had the sort of looks and personality that any girl would have killed for. Her only problem was that she always picked real louses for boyfriends.

'So, how are you doing?' she asked breezily, expertly changing the subject.

'Never had a better day,' he replied, as he took off his shirt and wrung it dry. 'It's good to see you again.'

CJ smiled in thanks – and when CJ Parker smiled she could outshine the sun itself. She clapped her hands together, suddenly the professional guide again, and walked over and introduced herself to Eddie and Shauni who, together with Hobie, were waiting by the large inflatable raft which would take them all downriver.

'OK, everyone get a lifejacket,' she said, and started handing out the bulky blue jackets to each of them. CJ knew that they were all expert swimmers, but it was senseless to take chances with the rapids. More than a few so-called expert swimmers had foolishly ridden the rapids without a lifejacket, and had drowned as a result.

As Mitch strapped on his jacket, he allowed himself a second to admire the scenery. Down by the crashing river there rose craggy cliffs, on top of which grew dark-green fir trees and pines. Beyond them in the early-morning mist, he could see a pair of eagles effortlessly sailing the wind currents, and even further still, the hazy blue silhouette of the San Bernardo

Mountains.

He could have been in another country, so different was this place from his home on the coast and the streets of Los Angeles. Even the air tasted somehow different, fresher and nuttier. Here nature ruled supreme in all its wildness, and beside it man faded almost into insignificance. They seemed millions of miles away from the corruption and crime of the big city.

'CJ, it's beautiful up here,' he said. 'You've just got to love it, haven't you?'

CJ glanced up from where she was helping Hobie with his lifejacket and smiled. 'I know it's beautiful – but I really miss the beach.'

'You should come back with us to Baywatch,' suggested Shauni.

Mitch nodded his head in agreement: it was a good idea, and might even take CJ's mind off her losing yet another boyfriend.

'The rookie swim starts next week,' he told her. 'Why don't you come and requalify? I'll get you a tower.'

CJ considered the idea for a second.

'I guess there isn't anything holding me here anymore, is there?' she said a little sadly as she remembered some of the good times she had had out on the river with Larry – even if the man was an unmitigated louse, she quickly reminded herself.

Satisfied that Hobie's lifejacket was fastened securely, she asked Mitch to pass hers over. As he did so, he asked: 'Were you kayaking on Troublemaker yesterday?' CJ nodded.

'We saw you,' said Hobie. 'You were awesome!'

'Thanks, Hobie. A little practice and you could be making moves like that in no time too.'

Eddie offered to help Shauni strap up her lifejacket but she brushed him off. 'It's OK, Eddie,' she snapped. 'I can do it myself!'

'Hey, I was only trying to help,' he muttered, and walked off to join Mitch who was preparing the raft for sailing.

'Eddie's pretty cute,' CJ said admiringly, after the lifeguard had left the two girls alone to put on their jackets. 'How long have you guys been together?'

'Two years next month.'

'Two years?' CJ was amazed. 'I've never made it that long! It seems like until then you don't have to worry about commitment. Then you've got to pull it all together, or it just slips away.'

'I know,' said Shauni bitterly. *And how!*

Meanwhile, Mitch had noticed the tension there had been all morning between Eddie and Shauni. While the two women were talking, he drew Eddie aside.

'So what's up with you and Shauni?' he asked.

'It's the Australian thing,' Eddie admitted awkwardly. 'She's all upset about it – and it's going to be all right, it'll work out OK ... I mean, it's not like it's the other end of the world, right ...'

Eddie suddenly realised that Australia was, indeed, the other end of the world. For the first time he discovered that he wasn't so sure about his trip, after all.

He quickly changed the subject: 'So what's with CJ? What's she all about?'

'CJ? Every two months or so the guy she's been dating breaks her heart,' he said, finding it hard not to resist a fond smile at the memory of some of CJ's more dramatic bust-ups with her boyfriends. 'Apparently the latest dude in her life, Larry, just dumped her. He took everything she owned – except the saxophone.'

'Wow, now that is brutal ...'

Mitch agreed, and shook his head. 'Left her with nothing ...'

'No,' said Eddie, remembering the out-of-tune wailing they had already heard this morning. 'I meant leaving her the saxophone!'

Chapter Seven

This was the ride of his life, Hobie decided, as CJ steered their inflatable raft down through the rapids. It was better than the time when his dad had taken him on the water-shoot ride at DisneyWorld, better even then that time they went skiing in the Colorado mountains. Shooting the rapids was the best experience of his life.

CJ guided the raft swiftly and expertly through narrow winding channels where the river's current buffeted them from side to side like dodgem cars at the fairground; and then in and out of foam-flecked rocks, dodging between them like an expert skier riding down a slalom run.

She knew the best parts of the river, where the rapids were fastest and roughest, and where you might be speeding along quite steadily when all of a sudden the river falls steeply away from you, and the current sends you flying off into space over a waterfall, to land with a heart-stopping crash in the boiling and turbulent waters below, before being swept along once again by the current.

Every time they shot over a waterfall, or turned a hair-raising corner so sharply that they all were nearly flung out of the raft, Hobie whooped with joy. So what if they were being tossed about by the river like a tiny pebble being skimmed across the water; so what if Hobie felt his stomach heave every time they hit a steep dip in the river or shot over a waterfall. He was having the time of his life!

When they finally reached a more placid stretch of water, CJ steered her raft full of exhausted passengers to the bank. Mitch leapt out and onto the firm ground again, which felt strange after he'd been rocked about so much in the raft, and took off his helmet. Even wearing it, his hair had been soaked, and it now hung in wet curls around his forehead. CJ thought it looked cute, which made Mitch hurriedly slick it back.

'Everyone OK?' he asked breathlessly.

'Sure, Dad,' Hobie replied, as Mitch lifted him out of the raft. Hobie's young face was glisten-

Father and son: Mitch and Hobie Buchannon (David Hasselhoff and Jeremy Jackson).

Nicole Eggert stars as rookie lifeguard Summer Quinn.

Summer's mother, Jackie Quinn, is played by Susan Anton.

David Charvet as Matt Brody.

Pamela Anderson as C.J. Parker.

Jeremy Jackson as Hobie Buchannon.

David Hasselhoff as Mitch Buchannon.

David Charvet as Matt Brody with David Hasselhoff as Mitch Buchannon.

ing with water and flushed with the exhilaration of just having discovered a brand new sport. Mitch had a feeling that Hobie's first ride over the rapids was going to be only the first of many.

'That was better than any water-park ride ever invented,' he said.

Following him out of the raft, Eddie had to agree: for sheer excitement and thrills, riding the rapids could even replace looking for the big 'dumper' wave to ride down at the beach. He helped Shauni out of the kayak; she was looking pale, and throughout the ride had been unusually silent.

'Hey, are you OK?' he asked in concern.

'Yes... No...' She shrugged and quietly slipped away from Mitch, Hobie and CJ, heading for a small clump of bushes a few metres away. She beckoned to Eddie to follow her.

'It was just like a roller-coaster ride!' gushed Hobie. 'Up and down, up and down!'

'Like most relationships,' CJ muttered, and drew Mitch's attention to the departing Eddie and Shauni. She and Mitch exchanged knowing glances: something was definitely up.

Hobie tugged at Mitch's sleeve and pointed to a pair of seedy-looking men on the opposite bank. They were crouched by the water's edge, swirling their prospecting pans in the water.

'That was the guy who taught me how to pan for gold this morning,' he said and waved at Drew. The mean-looking man grinned and waved back.

'Stay away from those guys, Hobie,' CJ warned. 'They're low-life dredgers. All they care about is gold, and they don't care if they screw up the river looking for it. You don't want to know them.'

Hobie nodded, impressed with the obvious contempt the normally easy-going CJ felt for them. He was about to ask her for more information on the two low-lifes when behind them Mitch suddenly gave out an unexpected whoop of triumph. They spun around.

'This is it!' said Mitch, and spread his arms out wide. 'I recognise this place!'

CJ frowned, wondering what Mitch was talking about.

'The secret spot?' asked Hobie excitedly, and ran up to his father.

'It's around here someplace,' insisted Mitch, suddenly feeling as crazy as a little child again. 'I'm sure of it!'

'Secret spot?' CJ was confused. 'What are you two talking about?'

'My uncle Alex left me something – I don't know what – in his will,' Mitch explained to her, and briefly told her the story of the will and its codicil in the envelope Chen had given him. 'It could be hidden around here someplace!'

'So let's go look for it!' suggested Hobie, practically.

He still had no real idea what Uncle Alex might have left behind but he bet that it was something valuable. It was left to CJ to point out that, not only did they not have the slightest idea what it was they were looking for, but they also didn't know where to start looking. Hobie's face fell, and even Mitch seemed crestfallen at CJ's display of simple adult commonsense. He walked slowly over to the edge of the river, and leant against a large dead tree.

'It was just about here where I caught my first fish with Uncle Alex,' he recalled. 'I remember, I was sitting just here by this tree when – hey, wait a minute!'

'What is it, Dad?' asked Hobie.

Mitch knelt down and pushed his hand through a hole in the trunk of the tree. When he'd been a boy Hobie's age he'd seen his Uncle Alex stash some of his fishing gear away in the tiny recess in the tree. Maybe, just maybe . . .

Yes, there was definitely something there!

He pulled out a small wooden box.

'We found it!' Hobie cheered, and jumped up and down with excitement. 'Well, c'mon, Dad, don't just sit there! Hurry up and open it!'

*

From their vantage point on the other side of the river, Lonny and Drew watched as Mitch pulled the box from the hole in the tree, and Hobie and CJ gathered around him.

'We'll just have to hold knives at their throats till they give us what we want,' Lonny said with relish, and stroked his wispy beard. He hadn't had a good fight in months: he'd love to take some of his frustration out on these squeaky-clean dudes from the beach.

'We don't know that they got what we want yet,' said his companion. 'We gotta chew this one up real slow. Think when to swallow – and when to spit . . .'

*

Unaware of all the excitement going on just a few metres away from them, Eddie and Shauni sat down together on an old fallen tree trunk in the small coppice. Shauni lowered her eyes to avoid looking directly at Eddie.

'I think you'd better prepare yourself for a shock,' she began ominously.

'What's up?' asked Eddie, his voice suddenly

full of concern.

'You know I've been nauseous in the morning lately?' she said.

'Yeah...' Eddie said and frowned. Somewhere in the back of his mind, he had a vague idea of what was about to come next.

Shauni took a deep breath. 'Well, I'm also three weeks late...'

Eddie brightened up. *That's a relief*, he thought. *Hey, if that's the biggest problem you've got then –*

He stopped dead.

'Hang on in there,' he said, slowly putting two and two together – or rather putting morning sickness and a missed period together. 'You mean you're saying that we're – you're – *pregnant*?'

Shauni nodded and then corrected herself, and shook her head.

'Well, are you, or aren't you?'

Finally Shauni threw her hands up in despair. 'I don't know, Eddie!' she blurted out. 'Maybe I am...'

'How? How is that possible?' asked Eddie. 'I thought we were being safe –'

'Nothing's foolproof, Eddie,' Shauni reminded him. 'Even the best precautions don't always work...'

For a few seconds they both sat in a stunned

and awkward silence, neither of them quite knowing what to say to the other, until Shauni at last stood up and said, 'I guess I should go back to the cabin ...'

'What?' asked Eddie, not hearing her.

The news had totally overwhelmed him, and a thousand thoughts tumbled one after the other through his head: Was Shauni pregnant or not? What did this mean for their relationship? How was this going to affect his year in Australia? Was it going to be a boy or a girl? Twins? What names should they give them?

Eddie felt numb. He couldn't make up his mind whether he should be feeling shocked or elated, so he simply settled for remaining confused. He looked up at Shauni, dimly aware that she had just said something to him.

'I'm sorry, what did you say?'

'I said I should get back to the cabin,' Shauni repeated patiently. 'If I am pregnant I probably shouldn't be rafting.'

'Fine.'

Eddie stood up and, when he found that his legs were shaking, thought better of it and promptly sat down again. He took Shauni's hand and stroked it tenderly.

'I'm sorry if I'm acting a little weird,' he told her. 'It's just that I'm shocked. This is gonna take me some time ... I think we should be sure before we –'

'What if I am pregnant, Eddie?' Shauni interrupted him and looked Eddie straight in the eye, demanding that he confront a whole load of questions he had never before considered. 'If I am pregnant, what happens then?'

Chapter Eight

'What is it, Dad?' asked Hobie as Mitch sat down on the ground and removed a single sheet of paper from the box. Mitch told him and CJ not to crowd him, and carefully unfolded the paper.

'It must be a map,' said Hobie knowledgeably, peering over his father's shoulder. Perhaps it was even a map to tell them where the Golden Boot was hidden!

He and CJ looked expectantly at Mitch, who frowned, looked back at them and then chuckled. He began to sing:

'In a cavern, in a canyon,
Excavating for a mine,
Lived a miner forty-niner –'

'Wait a minute,' said CJ, recognising the tune of the popular song about the Gold Rush. 'Those are the words to "My Darling Clementine"!'

'That's right,' Mitch confirmed and explained: 'Uncle Alex could never remember anything, so we always put things down in a song, because he could always remember lyrics!'

Hobie snatched the sheet of paper off Mitch, and began to sing the song using the words Uncle Alex had written down:

'In a cavern, in a canyon,
Excavating for a mine;
Lived a miner forty-niner
And his daughter, Lollipop.'

'*Lollipop*?' asked CJ. These sure weren't the lyrics of 'My Darling Clementine' the way her mother had taught her!

'It keeps getting weirder,' Hobie assured her with anarchic delight. 'Listen:

'Near the X, down in the clearing,
On the way to Devil's Mouth,
It was lost and gone forever,
Where the river's heading south.'

He looked at Mitch and CJ who both indicated that he should continue.

'Angle inland, towards New England,
To Tammy's Tree that's been cut down;
Grind the ground towards Wilma's Table,
If you're able, leap and bound.'

Mitch took the lyric sheet back from Hobie and sang the final verse:

'When you find it, and you've climbed it,
Teeter-totter to and fro;
Slide it off, and see the coffin,
And the Golden Light will glow!'

After Mitch had finished off the song (in more ways than one, CJ decided), they all three looked questioningly at each other. The song had to be about the Golden Boot, but what exactly did it mean?

CJ stroked her chin thoughtfully. 'You know there's a tree on a hill downriver,' she said. 'And it's tall, and has a round top . . .'

Mitch and Hobie looked at her expectantly. 'And?'

'– And some people round here call it the Lollipop Tree!'

'My darling Lollipop!' Hobie cried, and leapt to his feet. 'Let's go there!'

'Wait a minute,' said Mitch, who stood up. 'Eddie and Shauni aren't back yet.'

'Well, if we're going to go we have to leave right away,' insisted CJ. 'That stretch of river leading to the Lollipop Tree rises fast and it can get really hairy.'

'I'll go get 'em!' volunteered Hobie and ran off in the direction in which Eddie and Shauni had gone.

*

'Let's not tell anyone, OK?' said Shauni, as she and Eddie walked hand-in-hand back to Mitch and the others. 'I'd like to keep it private for now ...'

'All right,' Eddie agreed, 'but if you're going back to the cabin then I'm coming with you.'

Shauni shook her head resolutely. 'No, Eddie, I really need to be by myself for a while. We both of us could use some time to think. And you could probably do with some time with those guys ...'

'But Shauni, I –'

'Hey, shortie! Come on, hurry up!'

Hobie crashed through the trees and right into their tender moment. Eddie and Shauni smiled at each other: Hobie Buchannon had an endearing knack of turning up at precisely the wrong instant.

'My dad found the map to the treasure – well, sort of,' he piped up. 'We've got to go and dig up the Boot! Come on!'

Eddie raised his hands in a gesture of mock-defeat. 'All right, all right, I'm coming!' he said, and ran with Shauni down to the river's edge where Mitch and CJ were already pushing the raft out into the water again.

Hobie's face fell when Shauni announced that she wasn't going to accompany them on the journey.

'Aw, c'mon, Shauni,' he protested. 'If I'm not scared to raft then you shouldn't be!'

Eddie and Shauni exchanged a helpless look. 'What can I say, Hobie?' she said awkwardly. 'You know that I love swimming in the ocean – but not in the whitewater.'

'Hey, we'll go back to town, if you want,' Mitch offered. The Golden Boot had been hidden for some years now; it could wait another day, he reasoned.

'No, I'll be fine,' she insisted. 'You guys go off and find the Boot and have fun.'

CJ handed Shauni the small radio-phone she'd just been speaking into. 'I've contacted Jim and he knows exactly where you are,' she explained. 'He's going to four-wheel in here to get you. Wait for him here in the meantime, and if you need him just call him – the number's on the back of the phone. OK?'

Shauni took the phone, and thanked CJ, even though she wasn't anticipating any trouble. The river and the surrounding forest had a calming affect on her; she supposed it must be because of its distance from any sort of civilisation and the hurly-burly of the big city. And the two men on the opposite bank seemed to have disappeared. The boys and CJ could go off on their big adventure, she decided; she was just going to stay here and get some well-deserved rest.

While Mitch, CJ and Hobie were clambering into the raft, Eddie came up to Shauni and clasped her hands in his.

'I love you,' he whispered.

'I love you too ...'

Eddie kissed her tenderly on the forehead and then moved away, down towards the riverbank. 'See you.'

'Be careful,' she told him, and then waved goodbye to the others on the raft. 'You guys be careful too!'

Mitch looked curiously at Eddie as he stepped onto the raft. Something important had happened between them, he decided: Mitch hadn't seen Eddie being so openly romantic in quite a long time. When they got a moment together he'd ask Eddie what it was.

As they prepared to pull away from the shore and make off down the river they were unaware that they were being watched. While Lonny and Drew were no longer visible on the opposite bank, they still had Mitch and his friends firmly in their sights.

'They're going back onto the river,' whispered Drew, from their hiding place behind a large boulder on the opposite bank. 'Come on, let's get in the kayak and get after them.'

Lonny held him back. 'Wait,' he hissed, and pointed meaningfully at the lone figure of

Shauni. Already a plan was forming in his mind.

Back on the raft, CJ was finally satisfied that everything was in order, and that everyone was wearing their lifejackets. 'All right, you guys,' she ordered, 'helmets on!'

With a mighty push from Mitch and CJ, the raft sailed off down the river, following the current which would lead them to the largest gold nugget in the county.

On the bank Shauni waited until the raft had disappeared from sight around a bend in the river, and then she turned to wander back up the bank. She'd better make the most of her time in the country, she decided; tomorrow they would all be going back to the coast. She heard a slight rustling in one of the trees. Thinking it might be a squirrel she peered to take a closer look.

And found herself staring right down the barrel of a revolver.

Chapter Nine

Jackie parked her car in the trailer lot, and ran – or rather bounced – with joy up to the Oldsmobile which was parked at the edge of the trailer park, overlooking the sea.

'Summer!' she cried out, as she opened the door to the mobile home. 'Honey, what do you think?'

Summer glanced up from her copy of *Sports Illustrated* and looked at her mother. Jackie was beaming, and her joyful expression made her look even younger than she was. The effect, however, was somewhat spoiled by the fact that she was no longer wearing the blue dress she had had on that morning, but a tacky little black number which left very little to anyone's imagination.

'You got the singing job?' she guessed.

Jackie nodded excitedly. 'I did but –'

Summer looked enquiringly at her mom, as if to say: *OK, explain the dress. And it had better be a good story.*

'Like it's a singing waitress sort of thing,' her mother said sheepishly. 'In a sort of sushi bar thing ... We've got to wear this dress – it's a sort of uniform ...' She shrugged her shoulders, as if to say, 'Oh what the hell, that's California for you!'

Summer regarded her mother warily; she knew how much Jackie needed a job – she just hoped she hadn't landed one at some disreputable joint in Santa Monica.

'Mom, is this place sleazy?' she asked.

'No way,' Jackie replied adamantly, and, as way of proof, added, 'A lot of people from Malibu go in there ...'

'Mom, *I'm* going to Malibu High School!' Summer protested.

Jackie looked askance: she couldn't see what Summer was making such a big deal over.

'What if my friends' parents see you there?' Summer said in horror. 'That is gonna be really embarrassing! What if Matt sees you there?'

'Who?'

'Matt Brody, the guy I met today,' Summer explained casually, without mentioning the fact that she'd also met Jed. 'His dad's a big

Hollywood scriptwriter and they live up in the colony,' she said, referring to the exclusive enclave in LA, where many of the movie world's big names made their homes.

'Well, sweetie,' began Jackie with just a touch of rancour at her daughter's unthinking selfishness, '*we* don't live there, and *I* need a job!'

'Yeah, well, life-guarding pays fourteen dollars an hour to start,' replied Summer.

'That's why there are over two hundred applicants for just twelve positions,' Jackie told her, and stopped herself from pointing out to Summer that, even if she was a champion swimmer, she hadn't got the job as a rookie lifeguard yet.

As Summer shot her mother a don't-be-so-defeatist look, there was a smart knock at the trailer door. Jackie frowned: as far as she knew no one yet knew that she and Summer were in the area.

'Oh, that'll be Matt,' said Summer nonchalantly, picking up her beach-bag and walking over to the door.

'Good,' said Jackie. 'I'd like to meet him ...'

'No, Mom,' Summer said in horror. 'He can't see you wearing that ... that thing!'

'All right, all right,' said Jackie, admitting defeat and the fact that her new uniform was a little tacky even for California.

'He's come to show me some of his technique,' Summer explained.

'To show you some of his *what*?'

Summer sniggered. 'His *ocean* technique, Mom,' she reassured her and when Jackie admitted to being none the wiser, explained: 'Swimming, Mom, just swimming!'

And with that remark, Summer opened the door of the trailer – and found herself staring right into the face of Jed.

Chapter Ten

'We made it!' cried Hobie, patting his dad on the back.

'Hey, quit splashing!' he groused at CJ, as she and Eddie waded through the water to the shore, pulling the raft behind them.

'Look!' CJ pointed up to a tree on a small hillock in the distance. It stood tall and strong, and the leaves on its top looked just like a big green ball.

'That's Lollipop Tree,' she said.

Hobie whistled appreciatively. 'Wow, it really does look like a lollipop, doesn't it?' he said, and licked his lips just as if he'd found a real one. He rubbed his hands with glee: they'd discovered the first clue on the trail of the Golden Boot! They were on their way to fame and fortune!

'How do we get to it?' asked Eddie. The hillock

seemed a long way off.

'We get back on the river of course,' said CJ. By her side Hobie cheered: he hoped there'd be some real hairy rapids on the way to the Lollipop Tree.

'What's the next verse?' asked Mitch.

Hobie, who'd been invested with the all-important position of Official Keeper of the Lyric Sheet, unfolded the piece of paper, and sang:

'Near the X, down in the clearing,
On the way to Devil's Mouth;
It was lost and gone forever,
Where the river's heading south . . .'

'OK, then,' CJ said, ushering everyone back into the raft. 'All forward!'

The air exploded with the sound of gunfire. Bullets zinged all about them, pinging off the river rocks around them, and crashing into the water. The horrible, acrid smell of gunpowder filled the air.

'Quick, make for the rocks!' ordered Mitch, and they all began to paddle furiously towards a small rocky outcrop on the riverbank which would offer them some protection from the bullets.

'Where's it comin' from?' asked Eddie, keeping his head well down, and turning this way and that in an attempt to locate the source of the gunshots.

Mitch pointed up to a steep rocky crag about twenty metres away from them downriver. Lonny and Drew were positioned there, silhouetted against the late-afternoon sun. Their hunting rifles, aimed directly at Mitch's party, glinted menacingly in the sun. There was another familiar figure with them, and Eddie squinted in the sunlight to make her out.

'Shauni! They've got Shauni!' he cried.

His girlfriend was gagged and her hands had been tied securely behind her back. She looked terrified. Without a thought for his own safety he began to scramble to his feet, until Mitch pulled him abruptly down again.

'You want to get yourself shot?' he snapped.

'But Shauni ...'

'I know, I know,' Mitch said, more sympathetically but just as firmly. 'We'll get her,' he reassured his buddy. 'We'll get her!'

Lonny dragged a trembling Shauni forward to the very edge of the crag, and drew a revolver out of his pocket and placed it to her head.

'Do what you're told and no one gets messed up,' Drew called over to Mitch and his friends. 'Have the boy bring the song sheet over here!'

'No way!' Mitch shouted. He'd see Drew and Lonny in hell before he'd entrust his only son's life to scum like them.

'It's those dredgers,' CJ whispered to a suddenly very frightened Hobie. 'I told you they were no good.'

'They could be the guys who ransacked Uncle Alex's cabin,' guessed Mitch. 'They must have been following us all along ...'

'But what do they want, Dad?' asked Hobie.

'I would have thought it was obvious,' said CJ. 'They want to get their hands on the Golden Boot ...'

'Shauni, what are we gonna do about Shauni?' asked Eddie.

He didn't give a damn about who got the Golden Boot: at the moment he realised that the only thing he cared about in the entire world was Shauni – and the life of their unborn child.

Mitch slowly rose to his feet, shading his eyes from the sun so that he could see the crooks more clearly.

'OK,' he called out. 'You win. *I'll* bring you what you want. Only let the girl go first!'

Drew laughed scornfully, and glanced at his partner. They were no fools: Shauni was their trump card and they knew that Mitch or Eddie wouldn't dare to double-cross them while they still held her.

'No,' he said. 'The boy brings it!'

Just like all crooks, Mitch thought with

contempt. *Put a gun in their hands, and they think they can push anyone around. But deep down they're still the snivelling little cowards they've always been.*

'Hurry up,' cried out Lonny, and waved his gun threateningly at Shauni. 'Or we'll push her in the river!' Shauni looked down nervously at the river below her. Even if she could survive the ten-metre drop into its icy waters, with her hands tied around her back she knew she would drown within minutes.

Hobie stood up by Mitch's side.

'It's OK,' he said bravely. 'I'll go.'

'No you won't!' Mitch snapped. 'And get back down behind the rocks!'

'Mitch, c'mon man,' urged Eddie. 'We've got to do something before they hurt Shauni real bad!'

Mitch thought hard. Once the crooks got the lyric sheet they'd probably throw Shauni into the water anyway. There had to be a way for them to save Shauni, and stop the crooks from getting their hands on the secret guide to the Golden Boot. He looked around him for any inspiration. A few rotten pieces of wood, probably the flotsam from a wrecked canoe, littered the small rocky outcrop behind which they were sheltering.

Yes, there was a chance! It was a crazy scheme but it might just work! He selected the two largest pieces of wood and then began to take off his lifejacket and helmet, instructing Eddie to do the same.

'OK,' he said. 'Now this is what I want you all to do . . .'

*

CJ unhitched the emergency kayak from the raft's side, climbed in it and paddled out from behind the protection of the outcrop. She held up the lyric sheet, and prayed that the crooks wouldn't start firing at her.

'OK,' she called out to Drew and Lonny. 'I'll bring it to you.' She hoped her voice sounded steady: her legs were shaking like jelly.

Up on the crag Lonny looked at Drew, who nodded in agreement, and called for CJ to make her way slowly to them with the map. He glanced back at the rocks behind which the rest of Mitch's party were hiding; he couldn't see their faces, but he did spot the tops of their three helmets.

Satisfied that they weren't trying to trick him, he began to climb down the crag to the riverbank, and called out to CJ to meet him there, reminding her that if she tried anything smart Lonny would throw Shauni down from the top of the crag.

While CJ slowly paddled the kayak towards Drew, Hobie watched nervously. He wished Mitch was there to reassure him that everything was going to be all right, but his father had silently slipped out of the raft, along with Eddie. What Drew thought were Mitch and Eddie were simply their helmets, stuck on the end of the two sticks of wood. At that very moment the two men were swimming underwater towards the crag.

Trying to ignore the icy cold of the river, and with his lungs bursting, Mitch cut his way through the water with strong, smooth strokes. With any luck the crooks' attention would be focused on CJ and he'd be able to make it to the foot of the crag without being noticed.

CJ pulled slowly and deliberately up to the riverbank, and waited for Drew to come down to meet her. She cast a surreptitious glance up at the crag. Mitch had pulled himself out of the water, undetected, and was beginning to scale up the rocky face of the crag.

Finally Drew reached the river's edge and waved his gun menacingly at CJ. CJ returned the gesture with a steely look of defiance. *Just another couple of seconds now*, she thought. *Just another few seconds*... Carefully CJ stepped out of the dinghy, making sure that Drew's eyes remained on the lyric sheet which she held out tantalisingly for him. It was important that Drew keep his eyes on that lyric sheet; if he did that it was likely that he would not see Eddie who was swimming underwater, behind the kayak.

'This is what you want,' she said. 'Take it and let Shauni go!'

Drew was just reaching forward when he heard a sudden cry of surprise from above. The second his attention was diverted, Eddie sprang out of the water and threw himself upon him, sending the rifle flying out of his hand, and landing a vicious punch on his jaw.

It was Lonny's cry of surprise that Drew had heard on the riverbank. Mitch had finally reached the top of the crag, and had grabbed Lonny from behind, knocking his rifle out of his hand which fell the ten metres or so down into the river below.

Mitch rammed a fist into Lonny's fat belly, but only succeeded in winding him for a second. The bear of a man launched himself on Mitch with an angry snarl, knocking him to the ground. His burly hands reached for Mitch's throat, trying to throttle him. The man was enormously strong and Mitch felt suddenly dizzy as he was finding it difficult to breathe.

Summoning up all his strength, Mitch pushed the big man off him, and scrambled to his feet. For a second the two men looked at each other, like angry tigers deciding when and where to strike. And then, with an evil laugh, Lonny spun around and pushed the bound and gagged Shauni off the crag.

'*Shauni!*' Mitch cried, pushing past Lonny, who used the opportunity to make good his escape.

Mitch looked over the edge of the crag and saw Shauni's body falling. His eyes bulged in horror: if Shauni hit the water awkwardly, there was a good chance that she could break her back; even if she landed feet-first, as the lifeguards at Baywatch had been trained to do when diving into unknown waters, with her hands tied behind her back, she was going to drown.

Without a second thought, Mitch jumped off the crag after her.

Down on the river, Eddie also saw Shauni fall off the crag. In an instant, he was back in the river, racing towards her as she crashed feet-first into the water.

Angrily, Drew got to his feet and reached out for CJ, who smashed the paddle of her kayak over his head. He fell to the ground in a daze, and CJ leapt back into the kayak, making for the raft, before the criminal had time to recover.

Underwater, Shauni twisted and struggled in

her bonds. Drew and Lonny had done their job well: she couldn't loosen them even an inch. She felt herself sinking to the riverbed, her lungs filling with water, and she began to lose consciousness.

So this is what drowning feels like, she thought to herself. *Remember I love you, Eddie ...*

Before Shauni lost consciousness entirely, she was dimly aware of strong arms grabbing her. Frantic with worry, Mitch and Eddie dragged Shauni's limp body through the water and back to the raft. As soon as they reached it, Eddie lay Shauni on her back and pinched her nose while he attempted mouth-to-mouth resuscitation. A few painful, unbearably long seconds passed, and then Shauni started to cough and gasp.

Suddenly the air cracked once again with the sound of rifle fire. Drew and Lonny had regained their lost weapons and were firing on them. CJ dived into the raft just as Mitch and Hobie pushed it away from the cover of the rocks. They all grabbed for the oars, and began to paddle furiously down the river, trying to get out of the range of the gunfire.

Still Lonny and Drew kept firing on them, sending up spray as the bullets hit the water. It was a miracle that not one of them had been hit yet, thought Mitch; and then he suddenly realised that the gunmen weren't aiming at them at all.

My God, they're aiming at the raft! They're trying to sink us!

'Get her out of here!' he yelled at CJ, just as he heard an ominous *pop!* followed by an even more worrying hiss.

'They've hit the raft!' CJ realised in a panic. 'We're losing air!'

'Come on, faster!' yelled Mitch, as the raft began to speed off down the river.

Fifteen minutes later, and about a mile down the river, they moored by a small woodside clearing, at the foot of the hillock on which the Lollipop Tree grew. They had only just made it. The raft was losing air very rapidly now, and was in urgent need of repair. With Lonny and Drew behind them, they were safe for the time being, and they could all use a breather, before looking for the next clue in the song.

As Mitch and CJ occupied themselves with repairing the puncture, Eddie and Shauni went off by themselves down to a small secluded spot several metres down the riverbank. Hobie decided to wander off on his own to explore, after faithfully promising Mitch that he wouldn't lose sight of the raft.

Eddie was deeply concerned about Shauni:

having her life threatened by Lonny and Drew had finally made him realise just how much he really did care for her. Hell, two years was a long time: if he didn't know how he felt about their relationship by now, he never would.

'I've been doing some thinking,' he began awkwardly.

Shauni looked up, interested: there was something in Eddie's voice she had never heard before.

'I've been thinking about us,' he continued, and reached out for her hand. 'The thought of being without you for a minute – let alone a year – well, I just can't handle it . . .'

'Eddie, I've something to tell you –'

'Let me finish, OK?' he insisted gently. It wasn't every day that he found the courage to tell Shauni, or anyone, about his true feelings: he was determined that she was going to hear him out.

'I love you.'

He had said those three simple words many times before, but never before had he meant them as deeply as he did now.

'I don't think I realised just how much I do love you until I thought that I might lose you . . .'

'Eddie . . .'

'I love you,' he repeated with all his heart,

and took a deep breath. 'I love you and I want to marry you, Shauni.'

Shauni shook her head. 'I'm not pregnant, Eddie,' she said. 'I was just late, that was all. After all the excitement, well... The thing is you don't *have* to marry me.'

Eddie smiled gently at Shauni, and raised a hand to stroke her cheek. Didn't she realise what he was trying to tell her?

'You don't understand, Shauni,' he said. 'It's not because we thought you might be pregnant. I love you and I want to marry you. I want to have a family with you. And I want to spend every single day of the rest of my life with you.'

'Are you sure?' breathed Shauni and looked into Eddie's eyes. She smiled and kissed him on the lips. His eyes had told her everything she needed to know.

*

When they returned to the clearing, Mitch and CJ were putting the finishing touches to their repair job. Mitch looked up knowingly as Eddie and Shauni walked up to them.

'And what have you two been getting up to behind those bushes?' he asked flippantly.

Eddie looked down at Shauni. 'Go ahead – tell him!'

'Oh, nothing special,' she breezed. 'Just getting engaged . . .'

'Hey that's great!' Mitch rushed forward to shake Eddie by the hand, while CJ embraced Shauni.

'Hey, Dad, I found them!' Hobie ran up to them.

'Found what?'

'The X-trees!' he said, and started to run back in the direction from which he had come. 'Come on, let's go! Hurry up!'

As Mitch and CJ followed Hobie into a small clearing, Eddie and Shauni looked at each other and giggled. The second Hobie had announced his discovery Mitch and CJ seemed to have completely forgotten about their news. They laughed as if to say, *Some way to celebrate an engagement*! and then ran off after the others.

'See those two trees there,' said Hobie, when they were all together. 'What do they look like to you?'

Mitch looked at the two trees, which had been planted side by side. One rose up straight and strong, but the other, whose growth at some time must have been stunted, grew at an angle to its neighbour, and its topmost branches crossed over with those of the other tree.

'It's the letter "X",' he said, and patted Hobie on the back, impressed by his son's powers of observation. He wasn't at all sure that he would have noticed it himself; his Uncle Alex would have been proud of his great-nephew.

Hobie sang:

'Near the X, down by the clearing,
On the way to Devil's Mouth;
It was lost and gone forever,
Where the river's heading south ...'

'The river's heading south,' said Mitch. 'Hobie's right: it's the X-tree all right!'

'So what are we looking for now?' Shauni asked Hobie, who seemed to have suddenly assumed the role of leader of the Baywatch expedition to find the Golden Boot.

'Tammy's Tree, of course,' Hobie replied authoritatively.

'And what's Tammy's Tree?' asked Eddie.

Hobie recalled the words of the song: 'well, it's been cut down, hasn't it?' ... He looked around the clearing.

'It's got to be here someplace,' said Mitch and he suggested they all fan out to search for the fallen tree.

Within minutes Hobie had found it. Just outside the clearing, a large tree had been felled: too heavy to move, it had been left there and on its bark some lovesick Romeo had long ago carved the name of his girlfriend – Tammy.

They all cheered, caught up in the excitement

of the quest. They were definitely getting very warm now!

Mitch, CJ, Eddie and Shauni rushed up to Hobie, who was eagerly reading the next verse of the song. Mitch took the song sheet from him.

'Grind the ground towards Wilma's table . . .' He shook his head. 'Now what the hell is that supposed to mean?'

He looked to Hobie for assistance, but the boy stared back at him blankly: this one was beyond even Hobie's Sherlockian powers of deduction!

Wilma . . . Wilma . . . Eddie frowned: why did that name ring a bell with him? It wasn't as if he knew anyone called Wilma. He looked at Shauni, who was thinking the same thing as he. Suddenly they remembered. They were wrong: they *did* know one person called Wilma!

'Wilma Flintstone!' they both cried at once.

'What?' The others looked at them as if they had gone crazy.

'Remember *The Flintstones* on TV?' said Shauni.

'Wilma's table has gotta be some kind of a flat rock, right?'

Mitch nodded: he supposed it did make a weird kind of sense.

'A flat rock!' said Hobie. 'I saw some of them on the north fork of the river!'

'Well, what are we waiting for?' said Mitch. 'Let's go there!'

'See, Dad, it looks just like a table made out of rock!' crowed Hobie as he pointed at the large flat rock. Mitch consulted the lyric sheet again.

'When you find it, and you've climbed it,
Teeter-totter to and fro . . .'

He stood on the rock – sure enough, it moved beneath his weight! The rock had been placed there for some purpose: what could be underneath it?

'This has got to be it,' he said.

'Slide it off and find the coffin,
And the golden light will glow.'

They all gathered on one side of the rock and pressed the weight of their bodies against it.

'One –'

They all pushed hard against the rock: it didn't move an inch.

'Two –'

They pushed harder, their muscles straining and their feet planted firmly in the damp earth, to give them more leverage. This time, the stone moved a fraction.

'A little more,' groaned Eddie. 'Just a little more –'

'Three!'

With one final push, they heaved all their weight onto the rock. Slowly it began to move.

They pushed harder and the stone finally gave way.

It had been covering a hole in the ground, which led down into a long dark shaft.

'We found it!' cried Hobie. 'We found it!'

Chapter Eleven

In the phone box, Summer kept casting nervous glances back at the trailer as she waited for her connection to be made. From the trailer there came the sound of the angry voices of Jed and her mother; since he'd broken in to the trailer Jed was refusing to leave; he'd been drinking too, and that made him even more dangerous.

She drummed her fingers impatiently on the dirty glass window of the booth; the phone seemed to have been ringing for hours. Wasn't anyone at the other end going to pick it up?

'*Come on, come on!*' she said under her breath. '*Someone – anyone – please answer!*'

Finally, the connection was made: 'Hello, can I help you?' a woman's bored voice crackled across the line.

Thank God! 'Nine-one-one? Police?' Summer

said. 'My mother's ex-boyfriend has just forced his way into our trailer and we can't make him leave. You've got to do something.'

The disembodied voice on the phone told Summer to be calm. *Calm?* she thought. *How can I be calm? He might have a knife or anything!*

'My name's Summer Quinn, and we're at the Paradise Trailer Park, Number Thirty-Four,' she said, keeping her voice steady. 'Just send somebody around quick, that's all! We don't know what he's gonna do!'

She slammed the receiver down and ran across the tarmac to the trailer. Inside, her mother was sitting down, her arms crossed defensively over her breast. Jed was towering over her. Summer looked over at her mother; she was shaking with both anger and fear but was unharmed for the moment. Jed hadn't hit her, like he had done so many times back in Pittsburgh.

'I called nine-one-one,' she told Jed, spitting the words out at the man who had hurt her and her mother so much in the past. 'The cops are going to be here any minute now!'

Jed shot a hateful look at Summer, and snarled. She'd always been a sneaky one, had Summer, he decided, always going behind his back, resenting the influence he had with her mother. Hell, if Summer wasn't on the scene, he'd bet that Jackie would be back in his arms in a second.

'I ain't done anything illegal!' he claimed.

'Oh no?' said Jackie and rose to her feet. Now that Summer was back in the room she felt safe again, was able to stand up to the man who had made the past years such a misery for her.

'We're in California now, Jed,' she said. 'They have a stalking law here. And they enforce it! Keep harassing me and Summer and you'll land up inside!'

'There are other kinds of laws that apply to you and me, Jackie,' Jed said, shaking his fist at his ex-girlfriend. 'And I enforce those!'

'Jed, just get out of here!' Jackie pleaded, feeling close to tears. 'Just get out! We don't want you here any more!'

Jed growled: 'If I can't have you, Jackie, then no one else can!' He stormed out of the trailer, slamming the door behind him.

Jackie hugged her daughter. 'Honey, why didn't you tell me?' she sobbed, as she heard the sound of Jed revving up the engine of his car.

'I didn't want to upset you!'

'He's crazy, honey,' she said. 'He – Oh my God, what's that!'

There was a sickening *thud!* as Jed's car rammed into the back of the trailer. The trailer park was situated on the edge of a cliff overlooking the beach and Jed was pushing the trailer towards the edge. The trailer lurched forward and tottered precariously over the cliff.

'My God, he's trying to kill us!' screamed Jackie, and dived for the door of the trailer.

Outside Jed was laughing maniacally as he pushed the trailer further over the edge. Summer and Jackie leapt out of the trailer and ran across to Jed's car. Her face white with rage, Summer reached through the open window of the car, trying to wrest Jed's hands off the steering wheel.

'Summer, let go of him!' cried Jackie. 'He's crazy! Get away from him!'

Jed snarled and lashed out at Summer, knocking her to the floor, just as a motorbike roared into the trailer park. In a flash, Matt Brody took in the entire scene – the endangered trailer, the sobbing Jackie, and Summer lying dazed on the ground. He leapt off his bike, and wrenched open the door of the car, dragging Jed out. Jed landed a blow on Matt's jaw, stunning him for a half-instant. In response, Matt struck him in the gut and then gave him two well-aimed punches in the face.

Jed fell to the ground, and Matt launched into him angrily, struggling with him in the dirt. Blood poured from both their mouths, as they landed blow after blow on each other. But Jed was no match for the younger Matt, and eventually he lay slumped over, exhausted, on the ground.

Matt stood up and wiped the blood from his mouth, and heard sirens wailing as the police arrived.

As Jed was led away, Summer introduced Matt to her mother. Jackie looked approvingly at the young man. She might have her reservations about the motorbike, but there was no doubt that, when it came to picking her friends, Summer had undeniably good taste.

'Hi, Matt,' she said. 'Thank you so much.'

Matt smiled, as though saving damsels in distress was all just part of a normal day for him, and took Jackie's hand, kissing it in the way Jackie had only ever seen actors in European films do before.

'*Enchanté, madame*,' said Matt.

Wow, thought Summer's mother, *not only does he look gorgeous, he speaks fluent French as well!* If only she'd been fifteen years younger!

Chapter Twelve

Mitch and Eddie peered over the edge of the shaft, down into the blackness below. Behind them, Shauni held Hobie back; otherwise he would have been at the edge with his dad, and in his curiosity could easily have fallen in.

'I can't even see the bottom of this thing,' said Eddie.

Mitch picked up a pebble from the ground and dropped it down the hole. It was several long seconds before they heard it land with a muffled *thwump!* at the bottom of the shaft.

Eddie looked over at CJ who was already returning from the raft and carrying a long loop of rope and a large waterproof torch. Mitch took them off her.

'I'm going to go down,' he resolved.

Hobie gasped. 'Dad, you can't do that,' he

said. 'It might be booby-trapped!'

His father looked at him bemused. *Booby-trapped?*

Difficult, certainly. Dangerous, very probably. But booby-trapped?

'Haven't you seen *Indiana Jones?*' Hobie asked anxiously. Hobie had seen all three movies, and he remembered that every single secret pit Indy went down seemed to be wired with fiendish explosive devices, or at the very least inhabited by thousands of writhing poisonous snakes.

'I'll be all right,' Mitch reassured him with a smile. 'Besides, we can't come this far without checking out what's down there now, can we?'

Mitch took the rope from CJ and tied it loosely around his waist. Eddie tied the other end around a large rock, and then grabbed hold of the slack, and, with CJ supporting him, slowly began to lower Mitch into the shaft. The rope creaked and groaned, but showed no sign of giving way. The shaft wall itself was at a slight angle, so Mitch was able to swing out and use his feet to slow his descent.

As his eyes grew used to the dark, Mitch could see old wooden beams supporting the earthen walls; this shaft was man-made, possibly a disused and forgotten remnant from the gold-mining days of the last century.

Finally, after about a minute of slow and careful descent, Mitch felt firm ground under his feet. He tugged on the rope, and called up: 'I'm down.'

Mitch shone the torch around. He was in what appeared to be an old disused mine. Creaking wooden timbers helped to support the roof, and from somewhere far off in the shadows he could hear the distinctive tinkling sound of running water.

He untied the rope from his waist and bent down to examine the objects on the ground. If this has been a mine, it had obviously not been used for mining since the last gold rush in 1849: several rusted pickaxes lay amongst the dirt and rubble, but their wooden handles had long since rotted away. A few other objects lay abandoned on the ground too: shattered remains of elaborate vases and pots, and a small jade statue of Buddha who grinned inscrutably at him.

Hobie peeped over the edge of the shaft. 'What's down there, Dad?' he called.

'Some sort of ... crypt,' Mitch shouted back up. 'It could have something to do with the Tongs.'

'Is there a coffin?'

Mitch swept the crypt with the light from his torch. There, in the furthermost corner of the crypt, just as the song had said, was an old battered coffin. An oil lamp stood on top of the coffin and Mitch lit it with a match from a box he found on the floor.

'Do you see the Boot?' Hobie's voice echoed down the shaft.

'Not yet,' said Mitch, 'but there are lots of other artefacts ...'

Artefacts? Up on the ground Hobie turned anxiously to CJ. 'You don't think it really could be booby-trapped down there?' he asked.

CJ gave him a reassuring smile. 'No, Hobie, that only happens in the movies.'

Hobie breathed a sigh of relief: for a minute there he'd been really worried.

Down in the crypt Mitch placed the lighted oil lamp on the ground. Its flickering light cast eerie shadows on the crypt walls, as he removed the lid from the coffin. He peered into the wooden box, and then sighed with disappointment.

Well, what would you expect to find in a coffin? he chided himself, as he grimaced at the blackened pile of old bones. The skeleton was probably all that remained of one of the hapless victims of the Tongs, he thought. In the light from the oil lamp the skeleton glinted almost malevolently.

Glinted?

There was something else there too, hidden amongst that gruesome pile of bones! Excitedly Mitch plunged his hands through what remained of the skeleton's rib cage ... and he drew out a huge and heavy lump of gold.

'I've found it!' he yelled up to Hobie and the others. 'I've found it!'

'He's found it!' Hobie gave a shriek of delight, and in his excitement almost fell into the shaft. 'He's found the Golden Boot!'

'It's got to weigh at least fifty or sixty pounds,' Mitch called up. 'It's unbelievable!'

'Do you guys have any idea what that sucker is worth?' Eddie asked.

'It's probably worth millions,' breathed CJ.

'Yeah! We're all gonna be rich!' cried Hobie.

'I'm tying it to the end of the rope,' Mitch called up. 'Pull it up!'

Slowly Eddie heaved the heavy nugget up from the crypt. As the sunlight caught it, they all gasped with wonder. Shaped exactly like a cowboy boot, the nugget was huge, a beautiful freak of nature worth millions and millions of dollars.

'Alllll-right!' cheered Hobie.

'Can someone toss the rope back down?' Mitch's voice echoed irritatedly from below ground. Hobie, Eddie, CJ and Shauni looked at each other guiltily: in their sudden excitement they'd forgotten all about Mitch.

'OK, Dad,' shouted Hobie, 'it's coming down!'

'Leave the rope right where it is,' an angry voice commanded.

They all turned and saw Drew and Lonny who were covering them with their rifles. Drew nodded greedily over at the Golden Boot. 'OK, give it here.'

CJ hesitated, until Lonny unclipped the safety catch of his rifle. Reluctantly, she handed him the golden nugget.

Keeping a wary eye on the others, Drew ordered Lonny to replace the stone which covered the entrance to the crypt.

'You can't do that!' protested Hobie as the bearded crook sealed up the entrance. 'My dad's still down there! He'll suffocate!'

'Your old man's already in his tomb, boy,' sneered Drew.

Eddie made a move towards the crook and Lonny aimed his gun menacingly at him.

'The nugget's what you're after,' said CJ through gritted teeth. 'Just take it and go!'

'Yeah, and I suppose you won't tell nobody, will you?' scoffed Lonny.

Hobie looked despairingly at the sealed entrance to the crypt. *I can't let my Dad die down there!* he thought. *There must be something I can do!*

'We've seen how you folks all like river rafting,' Drew continued. 'So we're going to send you all off in your raft over the rapids. 'Course, we'll have to tie you up first . . .' Lonny took the rope which had been used to lower Mitch into the shaft and approached CJ.

Suddenly several things happened at once. There was a screech of tyres and a warning shot from a Colt .45 was fired into the air. Hobie grabbed a large stone and threw it at Drew, hitting him squarely on the temple, and making him drop his rifle in surprise. Eddie took advantage of the disturbance and head-butted Lonny in the stomach, knocking the Golden Boot out of his hands and onto the ground where it landed with a heavy thump.

'Sheriff Chen!' cried Hobie and ran over to the Chinese American who was already leaping out of his station wagon and covering the two crooks with his revolver.

'My Dad's trapped in the tomb! You've got to get him out!'

'Tomb? What tomb?'

'The Tongs! They buried the Golden Boot there. See we found it,' he said and pointed to the heavy nugget. He grabbed at the sleeve of Chen's sheriff's uniform. 'C'mon, Sheriff, we've got to save my Dad!'

Eddie walked up to the Sheriff. 'You've got to

arrest these two men for attempted murder and kidnapping,' he said.

Sheriff Chen looked at Eddie, then at the anxious faces of Hobie, CJ and Shauni, then at Drew and Lonny – and finally at the Golden Boot itself. The Tongs had been looking for that legendary treasure for years – and now here it was!

'So, someone's found the Boot at last.' He smiled and turned to Drew and Lonny.

Hobie looked at his friends: there was something wrong here. He had an awful feeling about all this, which was confirmed a moment later when Chen smiled at the two crooks.

'Good work, boys,' he said. 'Lonny, take the nugget to the kayak. And as for you four –' Chen waved his gun threateningly at Hobie and his friends, and gave a twisted grin – 'you four are going on a little trip down the river.'

Chapter Thirteen

Mitch looked up in despair at the sealed entrance to the crypt. A chink of light shone tantalisingly down at him from where Lonny hadn't quite covered up the hole – at least he wouldn't suffocate – but Mitch knew that even if he could scale the walls of the tomb, the stone's weight would be far too heavy for him to shift it, at least not without help from the surface.

He looked frantically around for any means of escape. Nothing. He examined the wooden timbers which supported the roof of the crypt; even if he could climb up one of them they were so old that they'd probably break under his weight, bringing the entire ceiling crashing down on him and burying him alive under hundreds of tons of earth.

No, he had to face it: he was trapped down here, with only the skeleton and the rushing sound of water for company.

Water?

Excitedly, Mitch searched for the source of the noise. It was coming from somewhere nearby. Suddenly he remembered what Chen had told him: there was an underground stream in these parts, which led out into the river! It was a slim chance, but it was the only chance he was likely to get!

He grabbed an abandoned pickaxe and began digging at the wall where the noise was loudest. The earth was hard here, and the muscles in his arms ached as he worked as though his life depended on it. Which of course it did, he reminded himself; but it wasn't just his life that concerned him. There was Hobie's life too: Mitch had to get out to save his only son!

Finally, he struck softer earth, and he dug harder, twisting and pulling his pickaxe as he tried to break through into the underground stream. A trickle of water seeped through the wall into the crypt. And then, as the stream found a new outlet, that trickle became a stream. And then as the pressure increased, the wall of the crypt collapsed as a gush of water poured into the crypt.

Mitch took a deep breath – the deepest breath

of his life – and threw himself into the oncoming torrent.

*

Chen, with Drew and Lonny's help, roughly forced Hobie, CJ, Eddie and Shauni into their raft, and made sure that they were tied up securely, back-to-back. CJ grunted as the Chinese-American pulled the final knot tight: there was no way that they were going to be able to move, let alone untie these knots.

The Chinese sheriff stood back, satisfied with his handiwork, and then instructed Drew and Lonny to push the raft back into the river.

Drew smiled. 'The current of the river will sweep them right into the Devil's Mouth.'

Chen nodded, and looked meaningfully at Drew and Lonny. Tied up as they were there was no way that CJ and the others would be able to prevent their raft from being dragged down into the swirling rapids of the Devil's Mouth: they would be smashed to pieces on the razor-sharp rocks, and their remains sucked down into the whirlpool, never to be discovered. Drew grinned evilly and he and Lonny pushed the raft into the river, where the current instantly caught it and started dragging it downstream.

Chen ordered them to put the Golden Boot into the kayak he had brought along with him in his station wagon. The sheriff had decided that it would be quicker returning to base along the river; Drew and Lonny could drive his station wagon back to town and anyway, he wanted to make sure that his enemies really had been eliminated.

'Where do you want us to meet you, Sheriff?' asked Drew.

'I'll meet you in Auburn,' Chen replied, as he put on his lifejacket and helmet and climbed into the kayak. He smiled. 'Good work, boys. You boys are going to be very rich real soon.'

Chen pushed off from the bank and started to cruise down the river. Drew and Lonny, their minds full of their future riches, had just started to walk over to the station wagon, when a sudden cry made them turn around.

Chen's kayak had overturned in the water; of the Sheriff there was no sign.

'What's wrong with him?' asked Lonny, expecting the kayak to resume its upright position at any second.

'He knows how to kayak,' said Drew, rushing down to the water's edge. 'There's something wrong out there!'

Briefly the sheriff's head surfaced, before an arm shot out of the river and dragged him down again. Chen surfaced again and thrashed wildly about in the water; he called to Drew and Lonny for help as his underwater assailant dragged him under for a second time.

Suddenly the kayak righted itself. But it was not Chen who was seated in it. Mitch grinned at the crooks on the shore, then sped off down the river, leaving Chen flailing about in the water.

'Stop him!' the sheriff howled. 'The gold's in the kayak! He's got the gold!'

Chapter Fourteen

For what seemed the hundredth time, the raft thudded sickeningly against the rocks, and carried on its unstoppable journey down the river. It was a miracle that it hadn't been overturned yet, or that none of them had been thrown out onto one of the needle-sharp rocks which lined this stretch of the river.

It was only by obeying CJ's shouted instructions, and by shifting their weight first this way and then that, that they had been able to steer clear of the most dangerous rocks which would have torn through the raft like a knife through butter.

The course of the water ran much faster now, and CJ knew they would soon be approaching the Devil's Mouth. It was a part of the river dangerous even for the most expert canoeist, and she realised now that this was where Mitch's Uncle Alex must have ended up, caught up in the merciless whirlpool and dragged down to his watery death. CJ had braved the Devil's Mouth once before and barely escaped with her life. Now tied and helpless, it seemed like this was going to be the end.

'Everybody lean left!' she cried, hoping against hope that their combined weights would alter the raft's course, and steer them clear of the rocks. It worked – for a second the raft did veer slightly to the left – but then the river took control again, and swept them on in its inexorable course.

'Hobie!' a voice cried out above the thunderous rush of the water.

Hobie looked back to the stern of the raft. There, behind them but catching up with them fast, was Mitch, paddling his kayak furiously in the crashing waters of the river.

'Dad, hurry up!' he screamed, then cried out as the raft hit a waterfall and was tossed up in the air, only to land with a sickening thud a few feet further downriver. CJ, Eddie and Shauni looked to the rear of the raft, and then back to the bow.

The entrance to the Devil's Mouth was no more than fifty metres away from them. Before it, the rapids thundered and boiled around the needle-sharp rocks which looked like hungry teeth ready to crunch their weak and defenceless bodies, and drag them down into the mouth of hell itself.

With muscles straining as never before, Mitch summoned up every last ounce of strength as he drove his kayak through the thrashing waters. It seemed he was gaining ground on the out-of-control raft, when a sudden cross-current caught him off-balance and the kayak capsized.

'Dad!' Hobie cried out.

Dazed for a moment, Mitch forced himself to remain conscious under the water, and with an almighty effort, performed a perfect Eskimo roll. On the raft, Hobie screamed his encouragement.

Through eyes half-blinded by spray, Mitch gauged the distance between him and the wayward raft. Only a few more metres to go. With a grunt, he ploughed on further, blanking out the pain he felt throughout his battered body.

He was almost beside the raft now.

The Devil's Mouth was only twenty metres away now.

Right, it's now or never! he determined, and let go of his paddle and grabbed hold of the side of the raft. With almost superhuman strength, he pulled himself out of the kayak and onto the raft. Hobie's cheers rang in his ears.

'Mitch!' cried CJ. 'Hurry! We're nearly there!'

The Devil's Mouth seemed to be grinning at them in welcome. Quickly Mitch untied first CJ and then Hobie, and then grabbed the paddles which Chen had left inside the raft. Furiously they rowed against the force of the current. Eddie and Shauni joined them, but it was no use. The current was dragging him in: there was no escape from the hungry rocks which lined the entrance to the Devil's Mouth.

Frantically Mitch looked around for a means of escape. There was a chance: a very small chance. If only the current didn't suddenly alter its course . . .

'Put your helmets on everyone!' bellowed Mitch, as the raft bounced from rock to rock on its way to the whirlpool.

With a bone-jarring *crack!* the raft was smashed against a large cluster of rocks directly in front of the Devil's Mouth. For one glorious half-instant it stayed there, until the current swept it on again. Taking full advantage of that half-instant they all jumped out of the raft, on Mitch's order, and onto the rocks. With aching and bleeding hands they clung to the slippery rocks as the raft was dragged past them, into the maelstrom.

Mitch breathed a sigh of relief. 'Hobie? Are you all right?'

Hobie had scraped his cheek on the rock when he had landed but was otherwise fine. Mitch looked at the others.

'Everybody OK?'

One by one they all nodded.

'Look!' said CJ, and pointed to their raft, as the current carried it straight down into the Devil's Mouth. 'She's going down!'

'Where's the Boot?' asked Hobie.

'Right there,' said Mitch.

Hobie followed his gaze. 'In the kayak?'

'That's right,' said Mitch. 'In the kayak ...'

In awed silence, they all watched as the kayak, with its precious cargo, was smashed and splintered against the rocks, and surged forward in the turbulent current.

The Golden Boot was lost forever now, Mitch realised, claimed by the Devil's Mouth – which is where it belonged.

Chapter Fifteen

On a deserted part of the beach, CJ performed her early-morning aerobics routine and grimaced. She hadn't realised just how out of condition she was; the trip down the rapids hadn't helped her, and she swore that she had damaged muscles on that trip that she never knew she had. But if she was going to pass the first test for rookie swimmers today, she knew that she had to be on top form.

She stopped and looked at the golden sands of the beach and the rolling breakers of the Pacific. *God, it was good to be back*, she thought, and realised that this was her real home, the place where she truly belonged. It hadn't been a mistake to come back, after all.

Mitch walked up to her and cheerily wished her a good morning. He'd been on the phone to the police ever since they had gotten back home the previous afternoon and now had some good news for CJ.

'I just got word that they picked up Chen and his two accomplices up in Washington State,' he said. 'Looks like they were trying to row up the Chilliwack River to Canada.'

'That's great news,' CJ said, and resumed her exercises.

'We'll all have to go back and testify, of course,' Mitch continued. 'They're being indicted for murder and kidnapping.' He paused and then grinned. 'It's OK, you don't have to be intimidated.'

CJ stopped in mid-stretch. 'Don't worry,' she said. 'I'll testify.'

'I mean about warming up here by yourself, away from all those younger and stronger swimmers,' he teased. 'Y'know, those kids whose only goal in life is to beat you out of a spot on the rookie team.'

'They don't intimidate me,' she said, glaring at him.

Mitch beamed and slapped her amicably on the back. 'Good! Experience is the most important thing,' he said. 'Besides, you only have to finish in the top twenty to qualify.'

'And how many are there in the test today?' she asked.

'Oh, only two hundred or so . . .'

*

Three hours later, the beach was buzzing with excitement, as two hundred eager and hopeful young swimmers stood at the water's edge, nervously awaiting the start of the rookie test. Each one of them bore a number on their shoulders which served to identify them against the list which Mitch, as Supervising Lifeguard Lieutenant, carried with him on a clipboard.

Clint walked up to Matt who was in the crowd, oozing with confidence, and impatiently awaiting the start of the test.

'Why, Matt, I sneaked a look at the list,' he began.

'And?'

'And Bobby Quinn is Number Ten!'

'OK!' said Matt. 'Let's go and check their shoulders. I've got to see who this wonderguy swimmer from the East Coast is!'

Matt and Clint walked down the line of swimmers, checking the numbers on their shoulders. Eight . . . Nine . . . Ten.

Matt looked up.

'Hi, Matt.'

'Summer?' Matt spluttered. 'You're Number Ten? You're Quinn? *Bobby* Quinn?'

Summer nodded. 'Well, Roberta, actually, but everyone calls me Summer.'

Matt's jaw dropped as his macho ego suddenly took a severe denting. *This* was his major competition? *This* was the one Coach had said had won all the East Coast meets, and could beat him in the swim trials? A *girl?*

And, what was more, an incredibly cute girl?

Matt decided that working as a rookie lifeguard at Baywatch might be fun after all.

A whistle blew and Mitch gathered all the swimmers around him to explain the rules of the test. He indicated a series of brightly coloured buoys which were floating out in the ocean.

'You will swim around the first buoy and then the second one. Is that clear?' Two hundred nervous voices muttered their assent.

'Then you'll come through the checkered flag on the beach... 'When you come through the checkered flag you'll be given an ice cream stick.' Two hundred bemused faces looked at each other until Mitch explained.

'Don't lose it: that ice cream stick has the order of your finish on it.

'This year,' he announced finally, 'only the first twenty of you will qualify for rookie school.' He looked over at CJ who was warming up, and gave her an encouraging wink. CJ turned to the girl by her side.

'Let them trample each other in the rush to get to the finish,' she said. 'I've done this before ... You've got to pace yourself ...'

Summer smiled. 'Gee thanks.'

'OK, you all ready?' cried Mitch. Two hundred swimmers nodded their agreement.

'On the count of three, then. One –'

CJ glanced over to Summer. 'Good luck.'

'Good luck to you too.' She turned around and saw her mom in the crowd of spectators mouthing her a word of encouragement.

'Two –'

Matt prepared himself for his race into the ocean. Hell, he was one of the best! He was gonna make the rookie team if it was the last thing he did. Maybe then his dad would sit up and take some notice of him.

'Three!'

Two hundred swimmers ran and dived as one into the warm waters of the Pacific Ocean.

Taking CJ's advice, Summer held herself back as the more inexperienced swimmers pushed their way to the front of the race. By expending all their energy straight away, she knew that by the time they reached even the first buoy they would be tiring.

Following CJ's example, she propelled herself through the water with strong, determined and regular strokes, all the time keeping an eye out for the swimmers behind her, and increasing her strokes slightly when it seemed that too many were catching up with her. A sudden pain shot down her left side. *Oh no! Not cramp now!* She gritted her teeth and tried to shut out the pain. She was going to qualify for rookie school if it killed her!

Through the spray and foam churned up by all the movement, she caught sight of a familiar face just behind her. A look of steely determination on his face, Matt Brody was catching up with her.

CJ had been right; by the first buoy, Summer was among the forty or so swimmers in the lead. *Don't push it now, don't overstretch yourself*, she warned herself. *Don't let yourself get carried away. Nice and easy does it...*

She reached the second buoy. By now some swimmers had given up the race, unable to take the pace. On the beach, watching the race, Jackie was roaring her approval: it looked like Summer was going to make it.

Summer's feet touched sand and on aching and shaking legs she heaved herself out of the water and made her way to the checkered flag. CJ was ahead of her, and Matt slightly behind her. Heart pounding, and her lungs ready to burst, she ran past the flag, grabbing her ice cream stick from the lifeguard on the way.

As she passed the finishing post she flung herself onto the warm, inviting sand. She lay there for long seconds, trying to catch her breath and slow down her racing pulse. Only then did she sit up and take a look at her ice cream stick.

Please, please, please let it be under twenty-one, she prayed. *I don't mind it even being twenty, but please not twenty-one or over . . .*

Summer forced herself to look at the number on her stick, and a wide grin came over her face. She'd made it! She'd actually made it! She had actually qualified for rookie school!

She looked at CJ and Matt who had both come over to join her. 'Congratulations,' said CJ, and showed Summer the number on her stick. Matt grinned and handed his over to Summer.

The Baywatch rookie school had just gained three new members.

Epilogue

The waves lapped gently against the beach and the warm Californian sun flecked Shauni McClain's hair with pure gold as she whispered, 'I do,' and looked lovingly up into her husband's eyes.

Eddie smiled tenderly, and bent down to kiss her.

'Then I now pronounce you man and wife...'

There was an approving cheer from the crowd who had gathered on the shores of the Pacific to attend the wedding, and Eddie and Shauni burst into laughter as Mitch tried in vain to quieten Hobie down.

Then Mitch shrugged and joined in the cheering as well. What the heck? It wasn't every day that two of your very best friends get married down on the beach!

Eddie beamed down at his bride. 'Happy now, Mrs Kramer?'

Shauni didn't say a word: a kiss was all the answer Eddie needed.

*

'So how long will Eddie and Shauni be in Australia, Dad?' Hobie asked, as he strolled home along the beach with Mitch.

'At least a year,' he said.

'I'll miss them,' Hobie admitted. He'd shared some good times with Eddie and Shauni; he wondered if he'd find friends to replace them.

'The lifeguard competitions are going to be held down there next year,' Mitch reminded him. 'Maybe we'll go see them then.'

'That's cool,' agreed Hobie, and then looked accusingly up at his dad: 'Of course if we hadn't let the Boot go under we'd go there on a gigantic humungous yacht!'

Mitch laughed. 'Well, Hobie, sometimes you lose something that seems irreplaceable, only to have something better come along in its place.'

He looked out at the Pacific Ocean. In the surf a good-looking seventeen-year-old boy was helping to teach a girl how to climb aboard a surfboard. Mitch recognised both Matt and Summer from the lifeguard trials.

'Dad,' Hobie said, 'if we got really rich would you still be a lifeguard?'

Mitch turned away from the ocean. 'Absolutely,' he said, without having to think about it.

'How come?'

'Well, believe it or not, I'm too young to retire, and I can't think of any job I'd rather have ...'

'Yeah,' Hobie said philosophically. 'Me too ...'

'Wait a minute; you don't have a job!'

'Hey, being your son is a lot of work!' Hobie pointed out seriously.

'Really?'

'Sure. You get shot at, you go down waterfalls, your dad gets trapped in a crypt ...' He looked down at the tuxedo and winged collar shirt he'd been forced to put on for Eddie and Shauni's wedding. 'Plus you get to wear these stupid penguin suits ...'

Mitch ruffled his son's hair. He thought Hobie looked particularly smart in his outfit. Hobie looked at Matt and Summer playing around in the surf, and then gazed up cheekily at his dad.

'I'm going in,' he declared.

Mitch shook his head. 'In that suit? Oh no, you're not!'

'Oh yes, I am...'

'You're not going in, Hobie, insisted Mitch as Hobie ran off down the beach, and made for the ocean.

'Hobie, come back!' Mitch cried and started to give chase, just as his son reached the first waves on the shore and started splashing around in the warm ocean.

'Hobie, come back!' Mitch yelled despairingly. 'That tuxedo's only rented! Come on back!'

Matt and Summer watched, amazed, as Mitch and Hobie splashed around in the water, having the time of their lives.

Matt tapped the side of his head, as if to say to Summer that the hot Californian sun sometimes made people a bit funny like that.

Matt and Summer didn't know it then, but in the months to come they were going to be seeing a lot more of Mitch and Hobie Buchannon . . .

HOW TO ORDER YOUR BOXTREE TV NOVELISATIONS

BAYWATCH

☐ 1-85283-852-3	*Tequila Bay*	£2.99

BEVERLY HILLS, 90210

☐ 1-85283-671-7	*The French Rival*	£2.99
☐ 1-85283-680-6	*Beginnings*	£2.99
☐ 1-85283-748-9	*No Secrets*	£2.99
☐ 1-85283-749-7	*Which Way to the Beach?*	£2.99
☐ 1-85283-820-5	*Fantasies*	£2.99
☐ 1-85283-825-6	*'Tis the Seasons*	£2.99
☐ 1-85283-816-7	*Two Hearts*	£2.99
☐ 1-85283-875-X	*The Factfile*	£2.99

All these books are available at your local bookshop or newsagent, or can be ordered direct from the publisher. Just tick the titles you want and fill in the form below.

Prices and availability subject to change without notice.

Boxtree Cash Sales, P.O. Box 11, Falmouth, Cornwall TR10 9EN.

Please send cheque or postal order for the value of the book, and add the following for postage and packing:

U.K. including B.F.P.O. – £1.00 for one book, plus 50p for the second book, and 30p for each additional book ordered up to a £3.00 maximum.

Overseas including Eire – £2.00 for the first book, plus £1.00 for the second book, and 50p for each additional book ordered.

OR please debit this amount from my Access/Visa Card (delete as appropriate).

Card Number

Amount £ ....

Expiry Date ....

Signed ....

Name ....

Address ....